NOT OF THIS WORLD:
EMULATORS

GERRY GRIFFITHS

SEVERED**PRESS**

NOT OF THIS WORLD: EMULATORS

WWW.SEVEREDPRESS.COM

ISBN: 978-1-923165-03-8

ALSO BY GERRY GRIFFITHS

DEATH CRAWLERS SERIES

DEATH CRAWLERS (BOOK 1)
DEEP IN THE JUNGLE (BOOK 2)
THE NEXT WORLD (BOOK 3)
BATTLEGROUND EARTH (BOOK 4)

CRYPTID ZOO SERIES

CRYPTID ZOO (BOOK 1)
CRYPTID COUNTRY (BOOK 2)
CRYPTID ISLAND (BOOK 3)
CRYPTID CIRCUS (BOOK 4)
CRYPTID NATION (BOOK 5)
CRYPTID KINGDOM (BOOK 6)
CRYPTID FRONTIER (BOOK 7)

DEEP IN THE WILD SERIES

DEEP IN THE WILD: SABERTOOTH (BOOK 1)
DEEP IN THE WILD: DIRE WOLVES (BOOK 2)
DEEP IN THE WILD: HELL PIGS (BOOK 3)
DEEP IN THE WILD: TRIBESMEN (BOOK 4)
DEEP IN THE WILD: SURVIVAL (BOOK 5)
DEEP IN THE WILD: MONGRELS (BOOK 6)
DEEP IN THE WILD: MAMMOTH (BOOK 7)

STAND-ALONE NOVELS

SILURID
THE BEASTS OF STONECLAD MOUNTAIN
DOWN FROM BEAST MOUNTAIN
TERROR MOUNTAIN

NOT OF THIS WORLD:
EMULATORS

DEDICATION

For Chelsea Griffiths,
Always determined

1

ANYBODY HOME?

Ashley Sanders yawned, stretched her arms above her head and sat up in bed. She swung her legs out and felt grit on the bottoms of her feet as soon as they touched the hardwood floor.

Mitch, being the major culprit tracking in the sand, had once again neglected to vacuum the bedroom. It was a lost cause trying to domesticate her husband and getting him to participate in household chores.

But what could she say? She loved the knucklehead despite his slovenly habits.

Wearing her normal sleeping attire, a T-shirt and stretchy shorts, she ducked into the bathroom and when she had gone pee and brushed her teeth, she came out, wiped the bottoms of her feet and slipped on a pair of flip-flops.

Ashley walked out of the bedroom, her rubber footwear slapping the bottoms of her feet with each step. She headed down the short hallway, the wall space adorned with professional looking black framed and white matted outdoor photographs of stunning beach settings, colorful sunsets over the ocean, remarkable shots of marine animals and shore birds, all taken by Mitch.

She came into the main living area, which was the largest room in their single story oceanfront home. As the house faced northwest, they were able to get just the right amount of morning sun without fear of overheating the front room. More pictures were on the surrounding walls, many of Mitch collecting marine life out in the tide pools, some of Ashley and Mitch mugging at the camera.

Two giant aquariums occupied much of the room; the larger one acting as a room divider, the slightly smaller one positioned nearer the windows facing out onto the backyard patio. The bigger aquarium was six feet long by two feet wide and almost three feet high. As the 220-gallon tank weighed well over 1500 pounds, two-inch thick planks were strung across three tiers of cinderblocks supporting the weight, leaving ample space underneath for plastic bins containing equipment and supplies.

A bookcase with marine biology texts and a ship's bell for a bookend was behind the desk facing the larger aquarium where Mitch would sit recording his daily research on his computer when he wasn't observing the activity inside the tank.

Like everything in Mitch's world, his desk was a mess of notepads and loose papers with ringed coffee stains. The books on the shelves were stacked on top of each other despite their random size; untidily askew or leaning like so many dominoes about to go tumbling over in unison.

To dress the room up, Ashley had laid down a faux Persian throw rug in front of the tank. As there was no backdrop on the tank, a worn couch and two mismatching armchairs could be seen through the glass on the other side of the room on the step-up flooring where the cords from both the aquariums ran under to the power strip surge protectors so as not to be a tripping hazard.

Ashley picked up a cereal bowl off of Mitch's desk. He'd left a spoon and a tiny coagulation of milk at the bottom of the bowl. She walked around the end of the big tank, leaned forward, and took a quick peek through the glass.

A canister aerator blew a steady stream of bubbles into the saltwater, providing oxygen and creating enough of an underwater current to sway the green finger algae—much like a waving hand—grounded in the gravel at the bottom of the tank.

An amber-colored glass jar was on its side, rocking gently back and forth in the undulating water.

A hollowed-out rock the size of a bowling ball was in one corner. A few smaller stones were scattered about to look natural though there were a couple of weighted-down toys resting at the bottom, buoyant enough to float when disturbed: an eight-inch long humpback whale and an equally detailed dolphin Mitch had handcrafted out of driftwood.

"Hello?" Ashley said. "Anyone home?"

She knew better than to tap on the glass and waited for a moment. Ashley gazed about the tank but when she didn't see any movement, she muttered, "Guess not," and went into the kitchen.

She put Mitch's bowl in the sink and ran some water to fill up the kettle.

Two dog dishes were on the floor: one with a bone emblem on the face half-filled with water, the other an empty food bowl with the name DOUGIE.

After some tea and toast, she figured she had ample time to shower, get dressed and drive the short distance to work.

She popped two slices of bread into the toaster and went to grab the handle on the refrigerator to get some jam when she spotted the Post-it note Mitch had left on the door:

ASH, WE'RE OUT OF FRUIT LOOPS!

"Well, good morning to you, too," Ashley muttered, opening the refrigerator door and glancing inside. She couldn't help but laugh. "And while I'm at it, why don't I pick up some milk."

2

BEACHCOMBERS

Palmetto Beach wasn't a weekend-getaway where sun worshippers flocked to hit the surf and work on their tans because there were no sandy beaches to lie upon, only jagged rocks and tide pools. Most days the weather was extremely chilly, as the morning fog refused to dissipate until around two o'clock in the afternoon only to creep back ashore before nightfall.

The fact the small rural beach town was nowhere near any major state highway and there wasn't even a motel anywhere nearby also detracted tourists from paying a visit.

With a small population of 167—a ballpark figure as there had never been an official census survey that anyone could remember—the close-knit community enjoyed the tranquil pulse of anonymity.

Which is why Mitch enjoyed living in the peaceful town. That and it was the perfect place for a budding marine biologist. Every morning he would get up like clockwork before dawn, careful not to wake up Ashley. He made sure their Cairn terrier, Dougie, had his wet chow and water before Mitch had his traditional bowl of cereal before heading down to the natural breakwater.

It was a fifteen-minute stroll down a narrow dirt pathway through the waist high white-feathered tipped pampas grass to the water's edge.

This morning Mitch wore a gray hooded sweatshirt, cargo shorts and water socks, and was carrying a five-gallon bucket with a meshed lid.

Even Dougie had water socks on each of his paws to protect his pads from the sharp edged rocks, or heaven forbid, a painful, if not life-threatening, sting if he should accidentally tread on a sea anemone.

As an added precaution, the twenty-pound dog was also fitted with a waterproof harness that fitted snuggly around his chest and had a grab handle in case Mitch had to snatch Dougie quickly and haul him up before a tidal surge washed him out to sea.

Mitch could hear the combers crashing ashore on the boulders on the northern tip of the estuary. Overhead, white gulls keened and soared like circling vultures about to swoop down on a decaying lump of roadside carrion.

Reaching the tide pools, Mitch saw more shorebirds perched on the white-speckled guano stained rocks; orange beaked Caspian terns with black skullcaps; a long-billed albatross with broad wings, further out on a jetty.

An energetic group of sandpipers ran down a thin strip of wet pebbles as though there might be a tasty treat awaiting them at the finish line.

Mitch watched the incoming tide wash over the rocks and fill up the pools then recede back to sea only to repeat the never-ending cycle over and over. He saw a pair of sea otters out in the fog amongst the seaweed, floating on their backs with flat rocks on their bellies, using the surfaces to break open clams. A hundred yards out it was a completely different world down in the kelp forest below the surface where he often went snorkeling for abalone.

Like every morning, Mitch's mission was to gather up food for Harry and Dorothy. He'd brought a net in hopes of scooping up some young perch, along with a pry bar for dislodging mussels adhered to the rocks and there was always the chance he might dig up some oysters or clams buried in the sandy ocean bottom.

Mitch placed the bucket on a rocky ledge and stepped knee-deep into a watery impression the size of a kiddy pool rimmed with green sea grass rippling rhythmically in the ever-flowing seawater. The tiny ecosystem was thriving with fiddler crabs less than an inch in width. What was unusual about the species was that its left claw was as big as the entire creature and always reminded Mitch of the comic book character *Hellboy*.

He used his net to scoop up a scuttling 6-inch red crab and shook the crustacean into the bucket. He spotted a conch, picked it up, and when he looked inside the shell's aperture, he saw the sea snail retreat deeper inside the siphonal canal. Mitch added it to the bucket.

Knowing the crab would go after any fish Mitch caught, he decided to stick with crustaceans this time and captured three 4-inch Pacific rock crabs as they were large enough to feign off the red crab. He felt around the bottom and came up with a couple of good-sized clams. He debated if he should grab some brittle stars, as they were filter feeders and helped to neutralize waste in the tanks, but he figured the crabs would make a quick meal of the five-armed creatures.

With his bucket near full, Mitch stepped out of the water and went ashore. He had been so preoccupied gathering, he had forgotten about Dougie. When he glanced around, the small dog was nowhere in sight.

"Dougie! Where are you, boy?"

Normally, Dougie would respond with a yap but all Mitch could hear was the cry of the gulls and the ocean waves slapping over the rocks. It wasn't like Dougie not to respond, as the dog generally didn't venture off very far from Mitch.

"Dougie!" Mitch dropped the bucket so he could clamber atop a boulder. He scanned the immediate area, and that is when he spotted Dougie. "Shit, boy, what the hell are you doing?"

Mitch jumped down and dashed across the rocks, the jagged surface knifing up through the rubber soles of his water socks as he ran to his dog's rescue.

Dougie had a 9-inch dungeon crab by one of its back legs and was dragging it out of the water with his teeth; a smart move to avoid getting pinched by the menacing claws.

But that wasn't what had Mitch worried.

It was the seal lion belly bouncing out of the water about to lunge for Dougie.

Mitch raced over, grabbed the handle on Dougie's vest and darted out of the sea lion's path.

The sudden jerk had caused the crab's leg to break off in Dougie's mouth.

The dungeon crab wasted no time and quickly scampered between the rocks.

Having missed its opportunity, the sea lion turned its blubbery body around and waddled back into the water.

"Give me that," Mitch said, taking the crab leg from Dougie's mouth. "What do you think this is, a dog bone? And quit scaring me like that."

3

MEET AND GREET

Ashley drove past the Bioengineering Clinical Research Institute of Medicine granite sign on the hillock of manicured lawn and parked her Honda Civic in the small lot along with twenty other vehicles.

She turned off her engine and took a moment to admire the single level glass facade building, the surrounding eucalyptus trees and the overcast sky imaging on the reflective glass.

She had completed two grueling interviews, undergone a lengthy indoctrination on company policies the day before, and knew she nailed the job when Human Resources had her sign a binding confidentiality agreement never to share company business with anyone, not even close relatives or she could be liable for breach of contract.

Getting out of her car, Ashley gathered her purse and locked the door. She wanted to look her best on her first day, so she wore her favorite yellow blouse, a bleated tan skirt, and a sensible pair of brown flats.

She followed the walkway to the front entrance and stepped inside the lobby.

A security guard in a gray uniform was waiting for her as she came in. "Ashley Sanders?"

"Yes, that's right," replied Ashley.

"Hi, I'm Ralph Kennedy. I'm here to escort you in."

"Ah, thanks." As Ashley had never been given the grand tour due to the company's classified nature, she wasn't surprised someone would be there to meet her though she was half-expecting it to be her immediate boss or someone she would be directly working with. She doubted seriously if Ralph would be considered a co-worker.

Ralph turned and proceeded to the nearest door.

A holstered semi-automatic pistol hung on the right side of a thick black belt with added ammo clips, a mace canister, and a set of handcuffs. He wore a yellow Taser gun on his other hip. It was obvious Ralph wasn't the type to take any crap.

He ran his keycard through the reader and held the door open for Ashley.

"Thank you, Ralph," she said.

"You're most welcome, young lady."

They continued down a hallway and went into a conference room. A rectangular table with a mahogany finish was in the center, surrounded by ten cloth-padded chairs.

"If you'd like to have a seat," Ralph said, graciously pulling out a chair from the table, "Dr. Swanson should be right in."

Ashley gave him a smile as he left the room. She placed her purse on the table and sat down. She glanced at the underwater photographs, two positioned at different heights on each wall, which she knew Mitch would be envious. Other than that, the room seemed rather stark.

She heard footsteps approaching and looked over her left shoulder.

An attractive woman in a white lab coat entered the room. "Ashley?"

"Yes," Ashley said and stood.

"Hi, I'm Dr. Faye Swanson, department head and biomedical engineer of the laboratory where you will be working."

"Pleased to meet you, Dr. Swanson," Ashley replied, shaking the woman's extended hand.

"Sorry that I couldn't have been part of the interviewing process but I've been rather swamped, which is why I had Drs. Carver and Miller fill in. They were quite impressed with you."

"I have to admit, I'm still not clear on my duties, other than I will be assisting with the documentation on a special project?"

"A *very* special project, Ashley. One I know you'll be excited to be part of as we're on the verge of a medical breakthrough that will change the world forever."

4

TELLTALE MIDDENS

Mitch opened the gate for Dougie and went around the side of the house with his bucket and placed the pail on a picnic table bleached white from the salt air while the dog ran around the fishpond. The bottom was green with algae. A pump hummed, circulating the brackish saltwater.

Dougie pawed at the concrete edge, attracting Mitch's attention. He went over and looked down. "Not again." He had been stocking the pond with young rockfish that could have passed for orange koi—Japanese carp which were nothing more than supersized goldfish—and some silver kelp perch in the event something came up and he couldn't make his daily trek down to the beach.

He got down on his knees and churned the water with his hand.

All the fish were gone; even the sea snails.

"Damn raccoons!" It had been an endless battle discouraging the masked bandits from their nighttime invasions.

Mitch had vigilantly secured the garbage can lid with bungee cords and never left any scraps after barbequing that might attract the bothersome marauders. He had hoped the motion-detector floodlights positioned around the backyard would have been a deterrent to scare them away but it was obvious the bright beams only made it easier for them to catch the succulent seafood in the pond.

He went back to the picnic table, removed the meshed lid off the bucket, and removed a handful of mussels, which he slipped inside a vinyl bag so none of the water would drip out. He opened the sliding glass door and stepped inside.

The main room was humid because of the two large aquariums, which acted like swamp coolers, dispersing moisture in the air enough to cause the furniture fabric to feel damp to the touch.

Mitch walked over to the larger fish tank. He laid the vinyl bag on the throw rug and began unsnapping the clips that fastened a section of the tank's cover. He lifted and laid the lid flat on top of the other half.

"Morning, Harry." Mitch gazed into the tank.

The filtration system rippled the feathery hydroids rooted at the bottom of the tank, which resembled ferns swaying in a mild breeze. A leather starfish clung to the glass while half a dozen three-inch sand dollars with five petal-shaped loops on their circular shells claimed residency on the bottom.

Bubbles rose from the helmet of a six-inch tall sponge diver in one corner of the tank. Besides the three large rocks, each one with an arch, there was a jumble of children's alphabet blocks.

Mitch grabbed his cell phone off his desk. He took a quick succession of digital pictures. Later he would transfer the images onto his computer to compare them with previous ones to see what had changed in the aquarium, as he knew Harry loved to disarrange his habitat.

Pulling a chair over, Mitch sat so he would be eyelevel with the midden of discarded shells in front of the teaching blocks.

A single eye with a horizontal pupil stared out from between a K and an M block.

"Yes, I see you, too," Mitch said.

Now that he knew where Harry was hiding, Mitch stood and reached inside the tank. He removed some black mussel halves, a couple of open clamshells, and a small conch. He shook the water off and placed them on a towel on his desk. He emptied the catch from the vinyl bag into the tank then walked around and sat at his desk.

Mitch made notes on a pad as he examined the trash heap on the towel.

In the case of the mussels and clams, it appeared Harry had scraped his beak along the hinge of the shells so he could inject his toxic venom to weaken the muscles so he could pry open the clamshells and use his enzymes to digest the mollusks.

Harry had simply drilled a hole in the conch shell to get at the sea snail.

Mitch got up from his desk and went over to the other aquarium. Just like in Harry's tank, there was a midden of empty shells. The litter was in front of the large rock situated in the corner of the tank.

This time, instead of an eye, a tubular arm extended out of the borehole to greet Mitch.

5

LAB TOUR

Dr. Swanson stood by while Ashley stored her purse in her assigned locker and donned a white lab coat.

"I noticed on your application you went to Stanford."

"My husband and I both attended," Ashley said.

"Really. So you were both marine biology majors?"

"We were, but..."

"What?"

"Mitch only completed his first year."

"Why, if you don't mind me asking?"

"We realized we could only afford for just one of us to go."

"So he dropped out so you could get your degree?"

Ashley hesitated for a moment. "That's right."

"That husband of yours must really love you to make such a sacrifice."

"He does, but he's never regretted his decision. Mitch has always been what you call a self-learner. He'd rather be outdoors than stuck in a classroom. You should see our house. He must have every book ever written about oceanography. Once he gets a notion in his head he's like Dougie with a bone."

"Dougie?"

"Oh, I'm sorry. Dougie's our dog."

"Come, let me show you around the lab," Dr. Swanson said and stepped out across the hall. She unclipped the employee badge from the breast pocket on her lab coat and ran the card down the reader. The pneumatic door swung open allowing them to enter.

The laboratory resembled an exotic pet shop.

On one side of the room were scores of terrariums on long benches; the opposite wall, rectangular aquariums butted together. Separate workstations and lab equipment occupied the central area.

Ashley counted five technicians sitting at their desks. She spotted Dr. Doreen Miller who had introduced herself as the lead medical technologist when she had interviewed Ashley. The woman was in her mid-forties, black hair, with a dark complexion. She was leaning on a partition, talking with a young man seated at his desk, when she happened to glance Ashley's way, and gave Ashley a subtle nod.

Dr. Swanson led Ashley over to the first habitat. "All the animals in our lab have one or more incredible attributes. Would you like to guess what this one is?"

Ashley gazed through the glass and saw a green lizard blending in with the foliage, clinging onto the end of a wooden spire. "Well, I know it's a chameleon and they can change the color of their skin to match their surroundings."

"That is true. They also use pluripotent stem cells to reconstruct nerve cells, muscle, and tissue when regrowing amputated limbs."

"Like when a lizard detaches its tail to escape its attacker."

"Exactly." Dr. Swanson pointed at the next vivarium. "In there are half a dozen geckoes, all of which have shed their tails during different tests so we can see how long it takes for complete rejuvenation. Thirty days is about the norm."

Walking to the next habitat, Dr. Swanson commented on the green iguanas, and then the newts, all with similar abilities to regenerate missing extremities.

"So these animals are the basis for your research?" Ashley asked.

"In part. Let's go over to the other side of the room." Dr. Swanson pointed out some of the equipment and explained their functionality as they made their way to the long line of aquariums.

Ashley gazed into a 40-gallon tank. An adorable creature stared back at her. Its face was nondescript with tiny black eyes, a smiling pencil-thin mouth, and looked like a child's must-have toy. A couple more were swimming in the background. "Oh, my. You have axolotl?" The aquatic salamanders were phenomena found only in Lake Xochimilco near Mexico City.

"We've been performing intensive studies to learn more about their healing process and the protein that causes the cells of their epidermis to form blastoderm," Dr. Swanson said. "Believe it or not, this one has lost the same limb five times and it has grown back."

"That is incredible," Ashley said, following Dr. Swanson to the next tank with a dozen or more starfish.

"What can you tell me about these?" Dr. Swanson asked, sounding like a college professor quizzing one of her students.

"Well, they're certainly strange, seeing as they can live up to 35 years and don't have brains nor blood in their bodies."

"Anything else?" Dr. Swanson asked with a sly grin.

"Ugh, you mean how they suck onto their prey and push out their own stomachs to digest their food?"

"I know. Disgusting."

Ashley fielded more questions from Dr. Swanson as they continued down the row of aquariums.

How sea slugs were able to detach their heads and regenerate a new body.

That sea squirts, known as tunicates, could regrow their entire body from just one blood vessel fragment in a week's time.

"These animals have all been instrumental in our study of regenerative medicine," Dr. Swanson said, turning down an adjacent hallway that opened up into a broader area ending with a glass wall and sealed door.

"Is that another lobby?" Ashley asked. She saw a large foyer with a marbled tile floor and a string of doors spaced evenly apart.

"That's our Procedural Department."

Ashley gave her an inquisitive look.

"In there we have the best medical equipment you could expect from a generous grant: topnotch surgical room and state-of-the-art 3D printer, along with some recovery suites." Dr. Swanson smiled and shrugged. "Unfortunately, this area is off limits to all employees other than Drs. Miller, Carver, and myself."

Ashley wasn't sure why Dr. Swanson had bothered to include the Procedural Department as part of the tour if only to warn her it was a restricted area. Or maybe the woman just liked to gloat.

They went back and down another hallway running perpendicular to the lab area.

"My office, Dr. Miller and Dr. Carver's are down here."

"So what is behind this door?" Ashley asked, stopping in front of a pneumatic door twice the width of a normal entryway.

As if on cue, the door *whooshed* opened and Dr. Carver stepped out. Dr. Carver had been Ashley's other interviewer. If she had to guess, he was somewhere in his early thirties. He was congenial and had a thick head of blond hair touching his shoulders, which made him look like a heartthrob doctor from a television medical show.

He took one look at Ashley and approached Dr. Swanson. "What are you doing?"

"Relax, Jason, I'm just showing Ashley around."

"Not in here I hope."

"We'll talk later," Dr. Swanson said dismissively.

"Fine, but I still don't think it's a good idea."

Ashley watched Dr. Carver storm off and couldn't help feeling responsible for causing friction between the two.

"You'll have to excuse Dr. Carver, he's been dealing with some personal issues," Dr. Swanson said, escorting Ashley into a room the size of a one-car garage.

Against the surrounding walls were a multitude of aquariums teeming with strange life forms slithering in the water.

A foldable flatbed cart stocked with clear acrylic containers was parked in a corner.

Ashley walked up to the first tank.

At first she thought she was looking at a transparent jellyfish but then it didn't look like any marine coelenterate she had ever seen in her textbooks. "I'm sorry, but I'm not familiar with this species."

"That's because we created them in our lab."

"Do they have a name?"

"Emulators," Dr. Swanson said. "Put your finger up to the glass."

"But doesn't that frighten them?"

"No, not at all. Go ahead, it's okay."

"All right." Ashley placed the tip of her index finger on the cool glass.

An emulator swam over.

It didn't have a proper body structure but resembled more like a ragged piece of tissue ripped from a marine animal.

Ashley saw minute glitter-like particles coursing through its gelatin mass.

"Oh my God," she gasped when a tentacle attached to the opposite side of the glass, mimicking her finger like a mirror image for a split second before returning to its original shape.

6

HOW WAS YOUR DAY?

Ashley sat at the picnic table on the back patio and took a refreshing sip of cold beer that had been chilling in the ice chest. Mitch had surprised her by preparing dinner to celebrate her first day on the job.

Tonight they were eating on proper china instead of the usual Melmac plates.

A vase of lilies was centered on the red and white gingham tablecloth.

He'd cooked up some calamari steaks on the outdoor camp stove and prepared his homemade clam chowder. A cube of butter and a loaf of sliced sourdough bread were on a cutting board.

Any other time, Ashley would have found herself swept up in the romantic evening under the tiki lights. Instead, she was still unnerved by her experience in the laboratory.

"What's up? I cooked your favorites," Mitch said, staring at the untouched food on Ashley's plate.

"I'm sorry. I'm a little distracted." Ashley glanced down at Dougie, lying by her feet.

"You know, you never said how your day went?"

"It went all right."

"So? What do they have you doing?" Mitch took a swig of his beer.

"I'll be working on a program conducting clinical trials."

"Oh, yeah?" Mitch pushed his empty plate and bowl to the side so he could lean his elbows on the table. "What kind of trials?"

"I'm afraid I can't say." Ashley rested her bare feet on Dougie's back and kneaded his fur with her toes.

"What do you mean? You can tell me. I *am* your husband."

"Sorry, buster. I signed a confidentiality agreement. No can do."

"What is it? Top secret?"

"Even if I could tell you, you wouldn't believe me."

"Try me."

"Not going to happen."

Mitch reached into the ice bucket and took out a bottled beer. He popped the cap off on the edge of the table and placed it in front of Ashley.

"You really think getting me drunk is going to work?"

"It has in the past."

"Not this time. How are Harry and Dorothy?"

"Up to their usual antics," Mitch said. "Which reminds me, I do have some notes I should input on my computer."

"You want me to clean up?"

"Well, I did cook," Mitch said with a boyish grin.

"Very well. Just do me a favor. Next time you want to surprise me with a meal, use paper plates."

"Gotcha." Mitch jumped up and went inside the house through the open sliding glass door.

Ashley shook her head. She gathered up the plates, took them through the main room and went into the kitchen. Of course, Mitch had left a royal mess for her on the counter and there were dirty bowls and cutlery in the sink.

It took her half an hour to clean up and put everything away. She looked up at the clock on the wall. It was only eight o'clock. She was tired and wanted to get an early night and knew Mitch would want to stay up late, working at his desk.

But before she retired, she wanted to spend some time with Dorothy.

Ashley went out into the main room.

Mitch looked up from his computer. "Turning in already?"

"After I have some one on one with Dorothy."

"You're going to make Harry jealous."

"I doubt Harry cares if Dorothy and I share a little girl time." Ashley stepped over to the aquarium by the back windows facing out onto the backyard. She unsnapped the clips and folded the cover back. She placed the palms of her hands on the surface and wiggled her fingers in the water.

It didn't take long before Dorothy showed herself and propelled out from her hiding place. Her head was fully inflated. She swam up and affixed herself to the glass.

Dorothy inched up slowly and wrapped four of her eight arms around Ashley's left forearm.

"How was your day?" Ashley said, soothingly. She could feel the suction cups puckering, the receptors tasting her skin.

The octopus blew a jet of water from her funnel.

Ashley knew it had been a direct response as the cephalopod had superior auditory perception, well within the range of Ashley's voice.

This evening, Dorothy was especially clingy like she had been pining for Ashley.

"Do you think she's capable of affection?" Ashley asked.

Mitch looked up from his computer. "What? Like love? Why, because she has three hearts?"

"It makes sense when you put it that way." It took two hearts to pump Dorothy's blue blood to her eight arms, one heart to feed oxygen to her intelligent brain.

"Something to consider. Let me make a note." Mitch grabbed a pen and began to scribble on a pad. "Are octopuses amorous or do they just like to grope?"

"Be sure you get right on that," Ashley said. She carefully unwound Dorothy off her arm and fastened down the lid. "I'm going to bed. Don't stay up too late."

"I won't." Mitch took a moment to glance her way. "Oh, and Ash."

"Yeah?" Ashley said.

"Kick ass tomorrow."

7

BLUEBLOOD

Ashley didn't mind that her cubicle was the smallest and there was a table inside next to her desk, set up with a coffee machine, two short stacks of polypropylene cups, a plastic tray of tongue depressor style stir sticks and a basket filled with packets of sugar, powdered creamers and sweeteners.

At least it gave her an opportunity to chitchat with her coworkers whenever they came in for a refill and for everyone to get to know her. So far everyone seemed nice.

Dr. Swanson had left a note on Ashley's desk along with a loose-leaf folder containing technical research material she wanted Ashley to upload into certain computer files. The department head also left specific instructions if Ashley had any questions, she should ask Dr. Carver.

Which is why Ashley was heading down the end of the hall and knocking on Dr. Carver's door.

"Come in."

Ashley held the manila folder to her chest and opened the door.

"Ashley, what can I do for you?" Dr. Carver gave her a smile and closed the laptop on his desk. He had a window view of a stand of eucalyptus, an impressive collection of reading material on a bookcase that took up an entire wall, and what had to be a 100-gallon saltwater aquarium.

"Is that a blue-ringed octopus?" Ashley asked when she saw the creature in the tank.

"It is. I see you know your octopuses."

"I should. My husband and I have two of them. Ours are common octopuses. We call them Harry and Dorothy."

"And how did you come up with those names?"

"Mitch named his after Harry Houdini because Harry is a bit of a contortionist and is always doing a disappearing act."

"Clever," Dr. Carver said with a smile. "So why Dorothy?"

"I named her after Dorothy Dietrich."

"Sorry, never heard of her."

"Dorothy Dietrich was often called "the Female Houdini" as she mastered all of his illusions, even one that he didn't care to perform."

"And what was that?" Dr. Carver asked, sitting back in his chair.

"The bullet catch."

"What's a bullet catch?"

"A marksman would stand a short distance away and shoot a .22 caliber bullet into a metal cup inside her mouth."

"That's totally crazy," Dr. Carver laughed.

"She performed the stunt a few times and then stopped, figuring it was best not to tempt fate."

"Good to see she came to her senses."

"Anyway, does your octopus have a name?"

"He does. Blueblood. He's getting up there I'm afraid."

"So sorry to hear that." Ashley noticed Dr. Carver staring at the manila folder in her hand. "Dr. Swanson said if I had any questions, I should see you."

"Sounds like Faye."

Ashley detected a change of tone in his voice. "I just need some clarification on a few items." She handed over the folder.

"Sure. Please," Dr. Carver said, motioning to the chair angled in front of his desk. "Have a seat."

Ashley sat down and watched the octopus glide along the bottom of the fish tank while Dr. Carver reviewed the first page. She couldn't help wondering why the man would have such a dangerous creature in his office, especially when the blue-ringed octopus had enough venom in its body to kill an elevator full of people in less than 20 minutes.

8

CONSENT FORMS

After spending half an hour in Dr. Carver's office, Ashley went back to her desk and worked all the way through her lunch hour. Someone had turned off the coffee machine in her absence and left the glass coffee pot empty except for a few dregs at the bottom.

At first she suspected one of her coworkers but then she had to wonder if maybe it had been Dr. Swanson making sure Ashley wasn't interrupted while working on her assignment.

Ashley was just finishing up when Dr. Miller entered the cubicle.

"How is it coming along?" Dr. Miller asked.

Ashley stopped typing to give Dr. Miller her full attention. "I'm just about done."

"Excellent. The medical consent forms are all signed and notarized?"

Ashley held up three documents for Dr. Miller to see. "Yes, I have them right here for Don Lamont, Stan McMillan and Ellie Phelps."

"Good, I know they'll be excited to get started right away."

"It's terrible what happened to them," Ashley said, having read their reports and seeing pictures of what they looked like before and after their accidents. "Those poor people."

"I know, it's tragic. I can only imagine their pain and suffering. But now we have the capability to make that all go away."

"You really think that's possible after what they've been through?"

"Trust me," Dr. Miller said. "Their lives are definitely going to change."

9

DON'S STORY

Don Lamont was feeling especially chipper that morning. He had gotten up a little earlier than usual so he could prepare a nice breakfast for Macy before he set out for work. He was dishing up her plate when she came into the kitchen.

"Do I smell bacon?" Macy asked, rubbing the sleep from her eyes and plopping down at the dinette table.

"You do." Don carried her plate over and set it in front of her. He had gone all out making her a four-egg omelet, hash browns, bacon, sausage and toast. Instead of her usual cup of coffee, he had substituted a tall glass of orange juice.

"Oh my God, Don. You made enough to feed my entire preschool class. What are you trying to do, make me fat?"

"No," Don chuckled.

Macy shot him a look. "Oh, I get it. It's because I'm eating for two."

"Ding ding! Give the girl a cigar."

"I wouldn't let Dr. Meyers hear you say that if I were you," Macy said, Dr. Meyers being her obstetrician.

"I'll save the cigars for when the baby's born. Anyway, I better get going." Don went over and gave Macy a peck on the lips. "Enjoy your breakfast."

"Don't be surprised when you come home if I'm still sitting here at the table."

"I'm sure you won't have any problem wolfing it all down the second I'm out the door. Besides, those kiddies can't teach themselves."

"Drive safe," Macy said, picking up her fork.

"I will. Bye." Don grabbed his lunch pail and rushed out of the house. He unlocked the door to his truck, got inside the cab, and fired up the engine. He'd given himself ample time to get to work before his shift started.

What he hadn't counted on was the gridlock once he got on the freeway.

"Oh, come on!" Don rested both hands on the top of the steering wheel and stared out the windshield at the long line of unmoving cars in all four lanes. Every minute or so, the car ahead would inch forward then stop.

Don wondered if he should get out of the slow lane and make a lane change but none of them seemed to be moving. He tried peering over the roof of the car in front of him to see if he could spot the problem but there was a tall van blocking his view.

He hoped it might be construction work and the crew was getting ready to open up the lanes, or if it was an accident, it wasn't too serious and the vehicles would move out of the way so traffic could resume.

That's when Don spotted the pregnant woman standing on the shoulder of the road beside her car with a flat tire. She was looking up and down the line of motorists hoping someone would pull over and give her a helping hand.

"Oh, what the hell," Don said. He cranked the wheel, pulled onto the shoulder and parked in front of her car. He climbed out and walked back.

"Thank you so much for stopping," the young woman said.

"Glad to help. How far along are you?" Don asked.

"What?"

"Sorry, it's probably none of my business. It's just that my wife and I are expecting."

"Oh," the woman smiled. "I'm due in two months."

Don could hear sirens approaching. "Do you have a jack and a spare?"

"Yes, I believe so. In the trunk."

"Could you pop the trunk for me?"

"Sure." The woman pushed a button on the fob in her hand and the trunk lid lifted up.

"You better stand over there," Don said and pointed to the other side of the car away from the traffic.

"Okay." The woman walked around the front of her car.

Don leaned inside the trunk.

He found the jack and lug wrench mounted on the side panel.

Lifting the cargo mat, he saw the spare tire secured by a wing nut.

A siren blared with a loud whoop.

Don glanced over his shoulder just as a car pulled out in front of a speeding police cruiser barreling down the shoulder.

The cop car plowed into the back of the vehicle, shoving it forward and slamming into the back of the pregnant woman's car, pinning Don's left leg between the bumpers.

10

STAN'S STORY

As foreman of the punch press department, Stan McMillan was proud to say his employees held the record of days without workplace injuries within the company, and Stan intended to keep it that way. Every hour without fail, Stan came out of his office to make sure the operation was running smoothly and everyone was following proper safety protocol.

He had been particularly worried about a new employee that day, named John Bennett, who had been slow to catch on, despite Stan assigning his most knowledgeable worker to train Bennett.

After a couple of complaints by the trainer, Stan decided he better see firsthand for himself if Bennett was cutout for the job.

The punch press department consisted of seventeen 30-ton machines, most of them designed to form thimble-sized parts out of flat sheets of metal, the massive presses capable of extruding three-foot tall cones out of two-inch thick copper disks.

As the work area was extremely noisy from the heavy dies slamming down on the steel bedplates like pile drivers, each worker wore ear protection, sometimes making it difficult to hear anyone speak.

Bennett's trainer stood up from his stool when Stan came over. Stan motioned for the man to take a break while he sat to observe Bennett.

As safety precautions, Bennett wore a pair of gloves and had straps around his wrists so when he pressed his foot down on the floor pedal to operate the press, his hands would automatically be pulled clear before the hydraulic ram came crashing down.

A small cart was next to Bennett with a stack of aluminum strips to be placed one at a time under the hydraulic ram to punch out a specific part. Stan watched Bennett grab a sheet of aluminum and align it crookedly on the plate.

"No, you're doing it wrong!" Stan yelled.

Bennett looked at Stan and shook his head.

"You're wasting material!"

Bennett unsnapped his left wrist restraint and took off his ear protector. "What did you say?"

"I said, you're doing it wrong!"

"Oh!" Bennett reached under the hydraulic ram with his free hand to reposition the aluminum sheet.

"No, you idiot." Stan lunged and fell off of his stool, knocking Bennett aside but not before the man's foot came down on the floor pedal.

The hydraulic ram slammed down, pulverizing Stan's right hand into a grisly paper-thin pancake, spraying workers on either side in a crimson mist.

11

ELLIE'S STORY

Ellie Phelps bolted into the bathroom and locked the door.

She placed both hands on the rim of the sink and gazed at her bruised face in the mirror. She couldn't believe the young woman staring back with the swollen eye was once the same prom queen in her high school yearbook.

Ray had slapped her a time before but her boyfriend swore he would never do it again and couldn't apologize enough for lashing out at her when they had gotten into a heated argument. Ellie had felt partly responsible and let the incident slide even though she knew she would never forgive him.

But this time Ray had used his fist, the punch knocking her to the floor. She had never experienced such pain before. When he saw her sprawled on the carpet, he panicked, realizing what he had done and bent down to help her up.

Ellie knew if she continued to stay with Ray, his unexplained bouts of rage would only escalate. She never thought she would be a victim of domestic abuse. There was a time when she couldn't understand why some women remained in toxic relationships, refusing to leave a dangerous spouse or partner.

That is until she became that woman.

Ellie ran the cold tap. She gingerly splashed water on her face. Grabbing a towel, she dabbed the tender area around her eye.

The doorknob rattled.

"Ellie, open the door."

"No, go away."

"Come on, Ellie, I'm sorry. I promise it won't happen again."

"You said that before. Leave me alone."

"Ellie, please. *Unlock* the door."

"I can't take it anymore. This is the last time. I want you to move out!"

"You don't mean that. Open up. "

Ellie turned. Her trembling hand reached for the doorknob. She jerked her hand away. "I can't!" she yelled.

"You better come out or you'll be late for work," Ray said.

Ellie took her cell phone out of her back pocket and checked the time. If she left now she might make it on time for her shift. She was tempted to call her parents and tell them she and Ray were breaking up and she wanted to move back home. "I'm coming out." Ellie unlocked the door and came out of the bathroom.

Ray stepped back to let her pass. "Ellie?"

"I'm going to be late."

Ray came up from behind, grabbed her by the arm and spun her around. "So what's his name?" Ray snarled.

"Who? What are you talking about?"

"This guy you work with? What's his goddamn name?"

"You mean Clark? Is that what this is all about? Clark and I are just friends."

"Are you?"

"Ray, we work together, that's all." Ellie looked down at his hand squeezing her arm. "Now let me go."

"Fine, but you better not be lying to me," Ray said.

* * *

Ellie parked behind the fast food franchise where she worked and turned off the ignition. She opened the driver side door and swiveled around in her seat so she could put on her grease-incrusted work shoes. Donning her work ball cap, she grabbed her purse off the passenger seat and got out of the car. She roughed up the soles of her shoes on the asphalt so they wouldn't be slippery as she closed and locked her door.

Punching in the security code, Ellie went inside through the employee entrance.

She made sure the door locked properly before stepping into the tiny break room to put her purse in her locker. Making her way down the narrow passage, Ellie glanced in the night manager's office but her boss wasn't at her desk. Ellie figured she was up front helping with customers. A recent delivery had come in as there were boxes left in the supply room that needed to be put away properly on the shelves.

Clark came rushing back. "Ellie, thank God, you're here. We're getting slammed. Jesus, what happened to your face?"

"Nothing. I walked into a cabinet. Do you need me out front?"

"No, Dolores wants you on the fryers."

"Where're Donald and Ruth? Isn't it supposed to be their turn?"

"They called in sick."

"Are you serious?"

"Dolores is royally pissed. Don't be surprised if she fires them."

"She can't expect us to work double shifts."

"We can talk about it later. I've got to get back," Clark said and rushed back to the front counter.

Even though she loathed dealing with rude customers, she hated having to sweat over the deep fat fryers even more.

She checked the temperature gauges on the five fryers and the LED displays to make sure the filters were operating properly during the cooking cycles before she went into the supply room to grab a box of frozen produce from the industrial freezer.

When she came back she noticed a digital display on a fryer was no longer functioning. She put the box on the metal shelf in front of the basket inside the tub full of bubbling grease. Clark had mentioned something to Ellie about a thermal sensor being faulty and wondered if he had been referring to this particular machine.

She was about to don her rubber gloves and safety glasses when a splat of hot grease burned her hand.

"Damn it," she cursed, leaning forward to turn off the fryer.

The frozen box plunged into the 450-degree grease, splashing Ellie's face and the front of her work shirt.

She was in so much agony she didn't even realize she was on fire.

12

PANDORA'S BOX

Ashley walked in the front door and kicked off her shoes. She dragged herself into the main room, tossed her purse on the sofa and plopped down. She was stiff and tired from a long day sitting at the computer, inputting Dr. Swanson's handwritten notes into document files. She rolled her shoulders and stretched out her legs, wiggling her toes to get the kinks out.

"Mitch! I'm home!" She waited for an answer but heard only the filtration systems bubbling oxygen into the two aquariums.

Harry was nowhere to be seen, hiding or camouflaged somewhere in his tank.

Dorothy, on the other hand, was anchored to the glass like an anxious pet waiting at the front door for her master to come home. Ashley often asked herself how it was even possible and was always astounded by the octopus' phenomenal ability to manipulate 280 suction cups on each of her eight arms so she could creep across the glass.

"Imagine how clumsy we would be if we had that many fingers," Ashley remembered Mitch once saying.

Speaking of Mitch, Ashley got up from the couch to go look for him. She searched the house but he wasn't inside. Which meant, he must be in the back.

On her way to the sliding glass door, Ashley tripped over one of Mitch's sneakers and nearly fell flat on her face. "Damn it, Mitch! When will you ever learn to pick up after yourself?"

Irritated, she picked up the shoe. She was about to walk it back into the bedroom when she got a better idea.

Ashley went over to Harry's aquarium, unsnapped the lid, and dumped Mitch's sneaker into the water. "That'll teach you," she said, watching the worn footwear sink to the bottom. "Sorry, Harry."

She walked across the room and opened the sliding glass door. She saw Mitch outside, working on the fishpond. She slipped on her flip-flops by the door and went outside. "What are you doing?" she asked straight faced, happy with herself having set up her childish prank on her unsuspecting husband.

"I'm making the pond vermin proof." Mitch had erected a chicken wire enclosure over the cement fishpond. "Let's see them get through that."

"You really think that's going to keep the raccoons out?"

"What? Are you questioning my engineering ability?"

"Mitch. They're raccoons. If there's a way, they'll figure it out."

"So how was your day?"

"Nice segue."

"I thought so. Or are your lips sealed?"

"I spent most of my day stuck at my desk transcribing reports into a data file."

"Sounds exciting."

"It was sad actually."

"What do you mean?"

"You know I can't talk about it," Ashley said, knowing she was itching to open Pandora's Box and tell Mitch about the three pitiful souls scheduled for the clinical trials.

"But you know you're dying to. I can tell by the look on your face." Mitch put down his tools and walked over to the picnic table. He reached inside the cooler and took out two bottles of beer that had been chilling on ice. "You look like you could use a cold one."

Ashley sat across from Mitch while he popped the cap off of her beer and set the bottle in front of her.

"I signed a nondisclosure agreement."

"So you've said."

"I could get in serious trouble."

"Then don't tell me."

"You promise to come visit me when I'm in prison?" Ashley said, kidding, though it wasn't a joking matter.

"Only if they're conjugal."

13

MISSING FOOTWEAR

Mitch could feel something poking him in the back. He reached around and felt Dougie pressed against him. "Will you scoot over?" He glanced at the clock and shot out of bed. "Ash! Wake up, you're going to be late for work!"

"What are you saying?" Ashley asked groggily, her head buried under the covers.

"You overslept!"

Ashley threw off the blanket and sheet, staring at the digital clock on her nightstand. "Shoot, I forgot to set the alarm."

"Sorry, it's my fault," Mitch said. "I shouldn't have keep you up so late."

"Can you make coffee while I jump in the shower?" Ashley asked, rushing into the bathroom.

"Sure thing." Mitch grabbed his T-shirt and cargo shorts off the floor and threw them on. He looked around for his high-top Keds but could only find one sneaker. He dashed barefoot into the kitchen, almost tripping over Dougie as the Cairn terrier cut in front of him. Dougie bolted outside the moment Mitch opened the sliding glass door.

Usually, Ashley was the one who made the coffee in the morning, so it took Mitch a few seconds to remember which cabinet she kept the filters. After opening and closing the cabinets over the counter, he found what he needed and set up the coffee machine. A minute later he could hear the hot liquid dripping into the glass pot.

If he knew it was going to be this much of a scramble he would have nuked a cup of instant in the microwave.

Mitch glanced through the sliding glass door and saw the empty beer bottles left on the picnic table. They had sat up drinking and talking until almost midnight.

In a way he wished he hadn't pressed her into telling him about the accident victims that she had read about at work, knowing the sobering reality she might get into serious trouble for divulging what was supposed to be strictly confidential company business.

Ashley ran into the kitchen, her hair still damp from her shower. She was wearing a yellow summer dress and a pair of leather sandals. "Coffee, snap to."

"Coming right up." Mitch grabbed the pot and filled up Ashley's travel mug.

"Thanks," Ashley said. She gave him a quick kiss, grabbed the mug and her purse and darted for the front door.

"Hey!" Mitch shouted. "I seem to be missing a shoe!"

"Ask Harry," Ashley replied, rushing out the door.

Mitch was still holding the pot in his hand. He grabbed a clean cup from the drain board and poured himself some coffee. He put the empty pot on the hot plate and turned off the machine. He took a sip, wondering about Ashley's comment that he should ask Harry the whereabouts of his shoe.

He strolled into the main room and stood in front of Harry's tank. That's when he saw his sneaker resting on the bottom. "Very funny, Ash."

Mitch put his cup on his desk.

He unsnapped the aquarium lid and reached down in the water to retrieve his shoe. He held it upside down to drain the water out before replacing the cover.

"Really, Ash, now you're just being mean," he said, noticing the shoelace was missing, figuring she had unlaced his shoe before tossing it in the tank and it was something else he would have to search for.

Mitch looked in the tank and saw Harry unfurl his arms, releasing the floating shoelace.

"Holy crap, Harry. Did you just do what I think you did?" Mitch rushed over to his desk to document Harry's incredible feat. "Wait till Ash hears about this."

14

MEDICAL VAN

On her way to work, Ashley managed a couple of sips from her travel mug. After driving like a maniac, she was relieved by the dashboard clock she wasn't going to be late after all. But it didn't stop her from speeding through the parking lot and coming to a jerky stop in the only vacant stall, causing her drink to tip out of the cup holder and spill coffee all over her floor mat. "Great! Just great!"

Luckily, she had an old beach towel draped over the backseat when Dougie rode in the car. She reached back, grabbed the towel, and began mopping up the puddle of coffee under her feet. She had spilled on her sandals but wasn't too concerned, thinking when the liquid dried the coffee stains would blend into the dark colored leather.

A vehicle startled her as it roared by. She looked out her side window and saw a white passenger van with tinted windows pull up to the curb by the walkway stretching down the side of the building.

Knowing she had a couple of minutes to spare before she needed to go in, and somewhat curious, she remained in her seat and watched the van.

A tall man wearing a white uniform stepped from the driver's door. He walked around the rear bumper to the opposite side of the van and slid open the side door.

A man hopped out with a pair of crutches. His left leg had been amputated below the knee.

Ashley guessed it had to be Don Lamont.

Next, a woman got out. Ashley figured it was Ellie Phelps as her head was wrapped in bandages. She was wearing sunglasses and would have been a great lead as *The Invisible Woman.*

The front seat passenger climbed out, no doubt Stan McMillan, because he was missing his right hand.

Dr. Swanson appeared from around the corner of the building and walked up to greet them. They were too far away for Ashley to overhear what they were saying.

After a short exchange, Dr. Swanson escorted the three arrivals, and the driver carrying their bags, down the side of the building.

Ashley thought it odd.

It was almost as if Dr. Swanson were sneaking them into the building.

15

3D PRINTER

Don Lamont took a moment to appraise his suite he'd expect to find in a luxury hotel. The room was spacious with an adjustable bed, a nightstand and lamp, a three-drawer dresser, a pair of matching club chairs and a small sofa with a coffee table.

He was sitting on the edge of the bed, unpacking some things out of his travel bag when there was a tap at the door.

The door opened before he could invite the person in. "Hey, Don," Dr. Carver said. "I see you're getting settled in."

"I am," Don said.

"Are you ready to get started?"

"Right now?"

"No time like the present," Dr. Carver smiled.

Don grabbed his crutches and followed the doctor.

Dr. Carver opened a door and held it so Don could pass through.

The overhead fluorescent lights automatically came on illuminating an examining table, a desk with a computer and a refrigerator-sized 3D printer with a closed cabinet door.

"Do you need me to get on the table?" asked Don.

Before the accident, Don was always going to the gym regularly, which was why he insisted in staying in shape, concentrating on upper body workouts.

It was amazing how many more pull-ups a person could do when they didn't have a leg.

"That won't be necessary." Dr. Carver sat at the desk. He opened a drawer, took out a single 8 by 10 photograph, and held it up for Don to see. "I chose this one of you and your wife taken at the beach. It was the best image of what your left leg and foot looked like before the accident."

"And you can really make my leg look like that again?"

"If you like, I can even throw in the tan." Dr. Carver typed a few strokes on the keyboard and swiveled the monitor around so Don could see the image on the screen.

Don saw a three-dimensional wire frame model of a left leg and foot. "That looks like a crude CGI rendering."

"It's what I used to program the 3D printer. Believe me, everything is to scale."

Since losing his leg, Don had been doing his best to cope, refusing to add any more stress on his wife, Macy, struggling with postpartum depression after the birth of their baby, James.

It didn't make their situation any better when the construction company he had been working for couldn't take him back as his job was too dangerous for an amputee. Being the accident wasn't job related, Don was unable to file a workman's compensation claim and the bodily injury liability coverage check he received from his auto insurance paid only a fraction of the hospital costs, putting them further in debt.

So when he was contacted about the free trial, Don jumped at the prospect of getting both feet back on the ground.

"Would you like to see it?" Dr. Carver asked.

"You mean it's ready? You bet I would!"

Dr. Carver got up from the desk. He walked over to the 3D printer and opened the cabinet door.

Don couldn't hide his disappointment when he saw the clear mold of his leg, filled with a brown liquid. "I thought I was perfectly clear when I said I didn't want another prosthetic."

"Believe me, this isn't an artificial limb. When we're done, you'll be running marathons."

"What's that brown stuff?"

"It's brine."

"You mean like fish food?"

"That's right."

16

HUMAN GUINEA PIG

Stan McMillan waited in his room, wearing a hospital gown and slippers. He was nervous even though he had been assured the procedure would be painless.

But how did they really know when he was about to be one of the first human guinea pigs in their clinical trial?

Stan knew it was just a phantom itch but it didn't stop him from trying to scratch the back of his non-existent hand. Sometimes he swore he could wiggle his fingers. He couldn't count how many times he had turned over in bed to reach across his nightstand for a glass of water and nearly knocked it over with his stump.

Or how many times he dreamt of that moment he made his fateful mistake. Much of what happened was a blur, and was so traumatic his doctors told him his mind would forever block it out.

What they called a safety mechanism to his psyche.

But the one thing he knew he would never forget as long as he lived was the haunting screams of those sitting at their presses suddenly bathed in his blood.

He was so jittery, his right knee kept moving up and down. A bead of sweat ran down his spine even though the air-conditioned room was rather chilly.

Stan heard a knock and the door opened.

"We're ready for you," Dr. Miller said.

Stan was hesitant and stared at the medical technician.

"You have nothing to worry about. I assure you," Dr. Miller coaxed, standing in the threshold.

Stan sat forward but remained in his chair.

"Not having second thoughts, are we?"

"No, I'm just..."

"A little apprehensive, I know. It's understandable," Dr. Miller said in a soothing voice. "You've been through a lot."

And he had. The mental anguish, the bouts of self-pity. Wishing he had never hired Bennett in the first place. The painful recovery.

Knowing he was going to be handicapped for life.

If that wasn't bad enough, management was going to reassign him if he ever returned, as they didn't want his workers seeing their boss walking the floor with only one hand, a harsh and constant reminder of what happens when a person suffers a lapse in judgment.

Maybe it was time he stopped feeling sorry for himself.

Stan rose from his chair. "Let's do this!"

17

OFFICE POLITICS

Ashley was easing into her new job nicely and was especially pleased when some of her coworkers asked her to join them for lunch in the outside employee break area with a spectacular view of the oceanfront miles away. The sun was just breaking through the receding fog and the noontime hour was sweater weather.

"Hey, I'm so sorry. I lost track of the time," Ashley apologized to Sean Tanner, Libby Brown, and Curtis Zane sitting at a round table under an umbrella. They had been the first to welcome her aboard, taking the time to properly introduce themselves, and eager to chitchat while they grabbed a cup of coffee at the table by the entrance of Ashley's cubicle.

"No problem," Sean said. "Libby just got here with our orders."

Ashley had taken an instant liking to Sean, who was a bit nerdy with black curly hair and black-rimmed glasses. He had been working at the lab for three years. His frequent trips to the coffee machine made her think he might have a crush on her until he confessed he was a caffeine junky, which explained why he was so wired.

"Okay, who had the ham and cheese?" Libby asked, delving through one of the bags.

Ashley could tell right off Libby and her were going to be good friends as the woman wanted to know all about Ashley. Where she went to college. Was she married? Did she have any pets? Libby had been eager to share, telling Ashley where she had studied, that she was single, and had four cats.

"That would be me," Curtis replied.

Even though Curtis seemed nice enough, he was a bit narcissus with his good looks and gave her the early impression he was coming on to her by his sly innuendos, but she set him straight right away by making sure he saw the simple gold band on her ring finger whenever she brushed her hair from her face.

"Ashley, you had the tuna melt?" asked Libby.

"That's right."

"Sean, the turkey club," Libby said, handing out the wrapped sandwiches.

"Where are my fries?" asked Sean.

"In here," Libby replied and handed Sean a grease-stained bag.

"So how do you like working directly under Dr. Swanson?" Curtis asked, taking a bite out of his ham and cheese sandwich.

"She keeps me busy," Ashley said, knowing she should be cautious and not say something that might come off sounding derogatory and get back to her boss. That was the problem being new on the job; figuring out the office politics and making sure she didn't end up the subject of the gossipmongers.

"Better you than me," Curtis said. "She can be a tyrant."

"Just ask Dr. Carver," Libby piped in.

"What do you mean?" It was too late. Ashley had taken the bait.

"They've been at each other for the past month."

"Any idea why?"

"I can't say for sure," Libby said.

"I'll bet anything it has to do with the clinical trials," Sean said, shoving a few fries into his mouth.

Ashley debated whether she should mention seeing the test subjects entering the building but decided she better not. For all she knew, the information in their accident reports was privileged information and not intended to be shared with other employees.

The last thing Ashley wanted to do was cross a line with Dr. Swanson and give the woman a reason to fire her.

Curtis finished with his sandwich and shoved the wrapper in the bag. He took a slug from his water bottle and looked at Ashley. "Did she take you into the room?"

"What room?" Ashley answered.

"Dr. Swanson. Did she show you the project they've been working on?"

Libby and Sean leaned in to hear Ashley's reply.

"What, you've never been in there?"

"We were never given access," Sean said.

"You can tell us," Curtis said in a conspiratorial tone. "What did you see?"

"Nothing," Ashley lied.

Libby glanced at her cell phone. "Oh crap, look at the time. We better get back inside."

18

GIVE THE MAN A HAND

Dr. Swanson was already inside preparing when Dr. Miller brought Stan into the room and had him lie down on a padded surgical table on a hydraulic base.

"How are you doing, Stan?" Dr. Swanson asked.

Stan noticed Dr. Swanson wasn't scrubbed up and was wearing a lab coat. He gazed around. "Where's the surgical team?"

"There's isn't any."

"I don't get it. I thought I was getting a hand transplant."

"Even better. When we're done, it'll be just like your old hand."

Stan was somewhat baffled and blamed himself for not asking more questions when he had volunteered but then he figured maybe it was best he didn't know the gruesome details.

He remembered a coworker who had walked around with a prominent limp for the longest time. When he questioned the man, the man said he had been contemplating a hip replacement, but when he watched a video of the procedure and saw the top of the femur sawed off and a long post inserted into the bone, he declined having the surgery and decided he would deal with the pain.

"I'm going to insert an IV into the back of your arm." Dr. Miller rubbed an alcohol swab on Stan's forearm. He felt a little prick as she inserted the wire needle. A coupler was on the backside of the needle, which Dr. Miller attached to a connector to a line of clear plastic tubing stretching up to a bag hanging from a stand.

"What's that for?"

"We want you sedated during the attachment."

"But I thought I wasn't going under the knife."

"You're not," Dr. Swanson said. "It's just best you're not awake."

Stan didn't like the sound of that. He was beginning to wonder if maybe he should rethink this whole thing. But before he could voice a protest, Dr. Carver opened the door and came in, pushing a flat cart with something covered with a blue cloth.

"Maybe Stan would like to see his new hand before we begin," Dr. Swanson said.

"It's right here." Dr. Carver leaned down and took out a clear plastic hand.

"That's it?" Stan asked.

"This is the mold," Dr. Carver replied.

Stan felt his head getting fuzzy. He watched Dr. Swanson fit the plastic hand onto his stump while Dr. Miller attached clear tubing to the dozen or more nipples on the transparent hand. "What's...that for?" Stan asked, his speech slurring.

No one answered his question and kept on working.

Stan's eyelids were getting heavy.

Dr. Carver unveiled a large acrylic tank filled with a pulsating liquid. He turned on a switch and a pump began transferring the contents of the tank.

Stan looked down at the plastic hand while it began to fill with hundreds of tiny metabolic organisms.

And then he slowly drifted off, the odd sensation in his stump fading away as the emulators burrowed deep into the tissue, replicating a circulation system of blood, bone, muscle and flesh.

19

PRACTICAL JOKE

Ashley was rather busy throughout the afternoon, updating another file for Dr. Swanson, but not so she hadn't noticed that Sean, Libby, or Curtis had not come over once to get their usual refill before Ashley cleaned up the coffee station before leaving for the day. She wondered if the three had only invited her to lunch just so they could get her to reveal what she had seen in that room.

If that was true, she had changed her opinion about them and decided she would keep her distance for the time being. She didn't see the point in getting too chummy with people if the only reason they were befriending her was just to get information out of her.

She'd played it over and over in her head and came up with the same conclusion that it must have been the bright overhead lights reflecting the image of her finger off the glass on the tank and Dr. Swanson had been playing a trick on her. Either way, Ashley decided it was best not to say anything.

When she arrived home and walked into the house, she discovered that Mitch wasn't home. She went into the main room and saw a note on his desk, saying he had taken his truck to the shop to get some work done and he would be home before dinner.

Her feet hurt so she kicked off her shoes and sat down at Mitch's desk. She glanced down at his open journal and saw his latest entry. He had found his sneaker inside Harry's tank.

"Guess this means I'm busted," Ashley said with a laugh and kept reading. Mitch wrote when he removed the shoe from the tank, it was missing a shoelace and Harry had been the one to remove it. "I don't believe it. Oh, I get it. You left your journal open on purpose so I would read it and think this really happened. Nice try, Mitch. I'll show you."

Ashley got up from the desk and stepped over to the big tank. She could see Harry slinking along the gravelly bottom. As soon as Ashley lifted the lid and put her hand into the water, the octopus came over and wrapped two of his arms around her hand. "Hey, buddy. What do you say we play a little practical joke on your dad?"

The suckers puckered on Ashley's hand in response.

"Let's see." Ashley gazed down through the water rippling from the filtration canisters. "Oh, this is too good."

With Harry clinging to her one hand, Ashley used her other hand to arrange the reading blocks next to his den to read: **I M H A R Y**

Ashley lifted Harry a couple of inches out of the water and spoke directly to the octopus, "Wait till he sees what our little Einstein has done now."

20

ROOM WITH NO MIRRORS

When Dr. Miller opened the door to Ellie Phelps' suite, she found the young woman sitting in a club chair with her back turned.

"Thank you," Ellie said.

"For what?" Dr. Miller replied, stepping into the room.

"Not having mirrors."

"Believe me, once we're through, you're going to love looking at yourself."

"Am I?" Ellie swiveled the chair around. "You really think so?" She was wearing a strapless one-piece swimsuit and the bandages on her head had been removed.

Even though Dr. Miller had studied many photographs taken of Ellie after her accident, it saddened her to see the poor woman's traumatic wounds in person. It was a miracle she was even alive having received third-degree burns on her face, neck, and patches of her upper chest.

By all rights Ellie should have been dead, and would have been, if it weren't for her quick thinking coworker Clark, grabbing a fire extinguisher and saving Ellie from burning to death.

"Does it hurt?" Dr. Miller asked.

"Not as much as before."

Dr. Miller knew third-degree burns not only turned healthy human flesh into molten scar tissue, they also destroyed nerve cells, masking some pain.

Having seen a *before* picture of Ellie from a copy of her driver's license, it was difficult for Dr. Miller to imagine the creature sitting in the chair in front of her as being the same person.

Ellie's face was stretched tight, pulling the corner of her mouth up in a weird sneer, her skin so scarred it looked like melted leather. Both of her eyebrows were completely gone and would never grow back. The burns stretched down her neck and onto her upper chest, the grayish skin much like the thin membrane on a sausage, ready to tear with the slightest movement.

"Mind if I come in?" Dr. Carver said, pushing in a wheelchair.

Dr. Miller saw the pained look in Ellie's eyes, knowing the young woman was embarrassed by her disfigurement in front of the handsome doctor.

"Ready for your spa treatment?" Dr. Carver said with a smile.

Ellie turned to Dr. Miller for clarification.

"You'll see when we go into the other room," Dr. Miller assured Ellie.

Dr. Carver assisted Ellie into the wheelchair and the three went into a room down the hall.

An oblong glass tub was in the middle of the room. A large hose ran out of the side and was attached to a pump connected to a three-foot high acrylic tank tucked in a dark corner.

The doctors assisted Ellie out of the wheelchair and into the tub.

"Have you ever been to a mud bath?" Dr. Carver asked.

"No, but my parents have," Ellie replied self-consciously.

"Think of this as a mud bath without the mud."

"What Dr. Carver is trying to say," Dr. Miller interjected, "is you might feel a little claustrophobic when we first begin which is why we will be sedating you."

"We will also be putting a breathing tube down your throat and clamping your nostrils so no liquid seeps in," Dr. Carver said.

"You mean I'm going to be underwater?"

"Don't worry, we'll be monitoring you the entire time."

Dr. Miller prepared the injection and gave Ellie the sedative.

Once Ellie drifted off, Dr. Miller intubated Ellie by inserting an endotracheal tube down her windpipe hooked to a running ventilator before clamping her nostrils shut.

Dr. Carver stood by at the acrylic tank and watched the emulators schooling together like a single gelatin mass. "Faye calls them her aquatic healers." He glanced at the door. "Where the hell is she?"

"You know Jason, since we're alone, I have some concerns."

"She'll be fine," Dr. Carver replied, looking down at Ellie, fast asleep in the glass tub. "Hey, we're two for two. Don't jinx it."

"It's not that," Dr. Miller said.

"Then what is it?"

"How long do you think it will be before they'll want to go home?"

"I'm sure Faye will release them once we're sure there aren't any side effects."

"Don't be so sure. She intends to keep them here so she can continue her research."

"But that would mean holding them against their will. We could be setting ourselves up for criminal charges. She can't do—"

The door opened suddenly and Dr. Swanson stepped in. "Shall we get started?"

21

TWO BIRDS WITH ONE STONE

Mitch was fit to be tied.

After all the time he'd spent erecting the chicken wire to make the fishpond impenetrable, the raccoons still found a way to get in and ate everything. Which meant he would have to go down to the tide pools later to catch more fish and gather mollusks for Harry and Dorothy.

Right now, Mitch was sitting at his desk with his journal open, sipping his coffee and staring at Harry's tank. He had to admit he had been blown away when he first saw the children's blocks spelling out **I M H A R Y**.

Harry was extremely intelligent, maybe more so than most animals on the planet, but Mitch doubted very seriously the octopus was smart enough to arrange the blocks into a coherent phrase.

Even though he knew it was another one of Ashley's elaborate jokes, there was a part of him that really wanted to believe it had truly been Harry showing off his superb intellect.

Mitch looked down and saw Dougie sitting next to the desk. The dog had something dangling out of his mouth he had found outside in the backyard.

"What do you got there? Spit it out!"

Dougie dropped a half-eaten fish head on the floor.

"Stupid raccoons." Mitch wasn't about to give up his private war against the nighttime marauders.

That's when he got the idea that would not only solve his thieving raccoon problem but would also be a way to get back at Ashley, thus killing two birds with one stone. Mitch picked up the fish head, slipped it into Harry's tank, and walked down the hall to the bathroom. As there was a separate shower stall and a bathtub he figured what he was about to do wouldn't be that much of an inconvenience.

Mitch closed the drain plug, turned on the cold-water faucet and ran water into the tub until it was half filled. He uncorked the clear jar of sea salt Ashley used whenever she took a bath and sprinkled the dissolving white crystals into the water. "There, that should do it. Now all we need is some fish."

Mitch walked back out to the main room. "You coming?"

Dougie was already snuggling into his doggie bed for his afternoon nap.

"Suit yourself." Mitch went out the sliding glass door, grabbed a bucket and left for the tide pools.

22

SEEING IS BELIEVING

Ashley checked the time on her cell phone. She had only minutes before she would be going home. As always, after she was through uploading Dr. Swanson's files and saving her work, Ashley made sure to back up the data on a blue thumb drive memory stick and lock it up in her bottom desk drawer.

She had to admit she was feeling a different vibe than from her first day.

Curtis, Libby and Sean had been standoffish. She knew they'd been waiting until she left her desk or went for a bathroom break by the diminishing level in the pot and the empty sweetener or powdered creamer packets discarded next to the coffee machine.

Ashley decided to use the restroom before leaving for the day. She made sure her desk was locked and grabbed her purse. Thankfully, she didn't have to pass by the other cubicles, so no one saw her exiting the lab.

She went down the hall and ducked into the women's room. After she was through and washed her hands, she came back out. She was about to turn right and head toward the front lobby when something caught her eye from the other direction.

Ashley glanced down the corridor to make sure all the doors on either side were closed, which they were. The last thing she wanted was for the doctors to see her sneaking past their offices. Come to think of it, it did seem odd that she hadn't seen any of them during the course of the day.

She continued down the hall hoping she didn't look too conspicuous and hid behind a slim panel near the glass wall of the side lobby. She took a quick peek and instantly recognized Don Lamont and Stan McMillan. The men were dressed in white T-shirts, gray shorts and wearing black rubber shower shoes. They were having a discussion in the middle of the lobby with Dr. Miller and Dr. Carver.

Lamont was standing on two legs.

McMillan was gesticulating with his right hand.

A door opened and a young, beautiful woman—oh my God, it was Ellie Phelps—stepped out similarly dressed as the men, followed by Dr. Swanson.

Ashley backed away, not wanting to be seen, and hurried out of the building.

23

ESCAPE ARTIST

The fastener on the tank lid popped open, creating a three-inch gap big enough for Harry to extend one arm out then another. Soon all eight arms were attached to the glass outside the tank so the octopus could deflate the rest of his body and squeeze his head out.

As the octopus descended, the sensitive suction cups explored the different surfaces, tasting the slick, cold glass and gripping the pitted cement cinderblocks, sliding down the side of a plastic storage bin and being repelled by the petroleum smell.

Harry looked like an uncoordinated creeping blob navigating the throw rugs and hardwood flooring, each arm seeming to act out of conjunction with the others as though they had minds of their own.

The mollusk crept quietly across the room, but Harry couldn't escape the sensitive nose of the Cairn terrier.

Dougie sat up and spotted the octopus moving spastically into the hall. He sprang from his doggie pillow, dashed over, and stopped short of the octopus ambling sluggishly across the floor.

Barking insistently, Dougie bounced up and down on his front paws.

Harry ignored the annoying pooch and continued to rove.

Dougie kept pestering, wanting to play.

Harry made his way down to the bathroom door, ajar enough for the octopus to fit through.

Dougie grabbed a trailing arm in his mouth. He tugged but Harry refused to be pulled back out and the door slammed shut, leaving the severed arm to coil around the dog's snout like a serpentine alien.

Dougie ran frantically into the main room, shook off the writhing appendage, and dove back onto his doggie pillow.

24

BAD DOUGIE

As Ashley drove home, she kept trying to rationalize what she had witnessed in the side lobby. She couldn't get the images out of her head.

Stan McMillan articulating with his right hand that should have been a stump, waving it in the faces of Dr. Miller and Dr. Carver.

Don Lamont's leg had looked so real. Ashley figured it was either the best prosthetic money could buy or the doctors had discovered a way to attach and reanimate a cadaver's leg to a living human being.

And then there was Ellie Phelps' miraculous transformation. The young woman was no longer a thing to be shunned because of her terrible burns. Instead, her youthful skin was healthy like that of a newborn.

Ashley remembered Dr. Swanson commenting the institute was on the verge of a medical breakthrough. At the time, she thought the doctor was feeding her a line, but now she realized the woman was telling the truth.

When Ashley pulled up to the house, she noticed Mitch's truck was not in the driveway. She got out of her car, walked to the front door and went inside.

She entered the main room and almost screamed when she saw the octopus arm lying on the floor in front of Mitch's desk. "Oh my God!"

Her first instinct was to rush over to Dorothy's tank. She looked back and forth sideways until she spotted the octopus with an open clamshell, searching for a scrap of meat she may have overlooked.

After a quick tally, Ashley confirmed Dorothy had all eight arms.

Ashley went over to Harry's tank and saw the lid was not on right. After a thorough sweep of the aquarium, Ashley came to the conclusion the octopus had managed to get out.

She picked up the severed arm and looked at Dougie. "Did you do this? Bad boy! You know better than this!"

Dougie sensed her tone and cowered in his doggie pillow.

Ashley felt bad for scolding Dougie and said, "Okay, if you want to redeem yourself, show me where Harry went."

The Cairn terrier hesitated.

"It's okay, Mommy's not mad. See!" Ashley gave him a goofy grin.

Dougie climbed out of his doggie pillow and made his way slowly toward the hallway. Ashley followed and saw a trail of blue splats on the hardwood floor leading to the closed bathroom door.

She opened the door and was shocked by what she saw. "How in the world did you end up in here?"

Harry was in the bathtub, playing with the cork and open jar of sea salt floating in the water.

Two of his arms were coiled around the handles of the faucets while the others squeaked along the inside of the porcelain tub.

Ashley stepped inside the bathroom. "I can't believe you did this." She heard footsteps and turned as Mitch appeared in the doorway, holding a pail.

"Holy shit!" Mitch said.

"I know. Isn't this incredible," Ashley said. "He not only escaped from his tank, he came in and filled the tub with water, and dumped in my pellets of sea salt."

"Wow, what do you know," Mitch said.

Ashley couldn't help but notice the strange look on her husband's face. "So what's with the bucket?"

25

MALCONTENT

"Like I said, it's important we monitor your progress for our clinical study," Dr. Swanson said to Ellie, who was sitting on the couch next to Stan while Don paced the room.

"For how long?" Don said, crisscrossing the room like a nervous groom.

"Until I'm satisfied with the results."

"You didn't answer Don's question," Stan said. "How long are we going to be cooped up here? A week, a month?"

Dr. Swanson didn't say anything and stood up from the club chair.

"This isn't fair," Ellie said.

"All I can say is please be patient," Dr. Swanson said and left the room.

"Can you believe this," Don said, walking up and kicking the side of the sofa with his left foot.

"Easy there, sport," Stan said.

Don looked down and was surprised he had ripped through the fabric and put a hole in the couch, despite wearing only a shower shoe. He thought for sure he had bruised if not broken a toe. There was no redness or pain indicating he had injured himself, only an odd tingling. A few seconds later, the sensation went away.

Ellie reached over and picked up a hand mirror off the coffee table that Dr. Swanson had brought and gazed at her reflection. "I never thought I would ever want to look in the mirror again."

"Yeah, well, news flash, that's probably all you're going to be doing," Stan said, gazing at his right hand. He made a fist and was tempted to slam it down on the arm of the couch in frustration but he refrained from doing so. Instead, he flexed his thumb and fingers like he was exercising his hand in a physical therapy session.

Stan was still in awe how they were able to symmetrically match his new hand to look almost identical to his left hand, minus the imperfections. He no longer had the ragged scar on the back of his hand he had gotten as a kid trying to climb over a barbwire fence or the ugly fungus infection under his right thumbnail.

Don sat on the edge of the coffee table. "I know they have our cell phones but what's stopping us from just walking out of here?"

"Well, we're locked in for one thing," Stan replied.

"What do you mean? We have access in and out of our rooms."

"Have you tried the lobby exit doors?"

"No."

"You need a keycard to get out."

"So you're saying we couldn't leave even if we wanted to," Ellie said, putting down the mirror.

"Not unless we can get our hands on one of those keycards."

"You know, have you ever thought how we're going to explain all of this? My company already told me there was no position for me. What do you think they're going to say when I show up with this?" Don said, patting his left thigh.

"Don's right," Ellie said. "No one is going to believe I look like this after some cosmetic surgery."

"Or that I magically grew a hand," Stan said. "I'd say all three of us are screwed. Looks like we're stuck here."

"Not so fast," Don said. "I have a wife and baby boy."

"And I have a boyfriend," Ellie piped in. "Or at least I think I do."

"Oh, yeah," Stan said. "What's his name?"

"Clark."

"Well, I may not have a wife and kid or a girlfriend but that doesn't mean I don't have a life." Stan reached out and joined hands with Don and Ellie like they were teammates getting pumped for a big game. "Then I suggest we put our heads together and figure a way out of here."

26

NO LONGER SNUBBED

When Ashley got to work the next day, she found a small bouquet of flowers on her desk. She had no idea who they were from as there wasn't a card.

Could it be from a mysterious admirer? Maybe Curtis or Sean?

Or were the flowers just a show of appreciation for a job well done from one of the doctors?

Either way, she couldn't help but feel a little apprehensive not knowing who they were from.

"Good morning."

Ashley looked up from her chair and saw Libby standing just outside her cubicle.

"Libby, you are going to have to wait. I just got here and I haven't had a chance to make any coffee."

"I'm not here for that. I want to apologize for yesterday. If you must know, it was all Curtis' idea to snub you. He's been dying to know what Dr. Swanson has in that room. Well, to be honest, so have Sean and I. Curtis thought you might open up and tell us over lunch."

"I'm sorry, Libby, but there's really nothing to tell."

"Oh."

"So, I'm guessing *you* put the flowers on my desk?"

"Like I said, I'm sorry for the way I acted. I hope we can still be friends."

"That goes for me, too," Sean said, appearing over the cubicle wall.

"And me," Curtis said, popping his head up.

"Sure, no harm done," Ashley smiled, relieved they had cleared the air.

Curtis raised his empty mug for Ashley to see.

"Once I get settled," Ashley said, "I'll make a fresh pot."

"You're the best," Curtis said, and the three of them went back to their desks.

Ashley looked at the flower arrangement. The half-dozen yellow roses were already wilting and a few of the petals had fallen onto her desk blotter, which made Ashley wonder if Libby had originally bought the flowers for her place and decided no one would know if she pawned them off on Ashley.

She reached in her purse and took out her desk key. She leaned over to unlock the bottom drawer and found it open a fraction of an inch.

Someone had broken into her desk and stolen the blue thumb drive memory stick.

27

CHANGE OF PLAN

Stan and Don lingered before opening the door of Ellie's suite.

"Promise you won't chicken out," Don said.

"I won't," Ellie replied, sitting on the couch in her bathrobe.

"We're counting on you, Ellie," Stan said. "You want to see that boyfriend of yours, don't you?"

"Of course."

"Then you know what you have to do."

"Good luck," Don said, "you can do this."

Before Ellie could say another word, Stan and Don were out the door and going back to their rooms. She didn't want to disappoint them but she still wasn't sure she could pull off seducing Dr. Carver.

Sure he was handsome and she was a young good-looking woman but that didn't necessarily mean he would be attracted to her once she came on to him.

And then there was crossing the line of the doctor/patient fraternizing thing.

Not to mention how Clark would react once she told him how she had tricked her doctor into believing they could have a romantic relationship if he allowed her to leave.

The more she thought about the consequences the more she was certain she had changed her mind. No, there had to be another way.

She heard a light tap at the door.

"Come in."

Dr. Carver opened the door. "I know I'm a couple of minutes early but I was anxious to see how you were doing?"

"All right, I guess," Ellie said.

Dr. Carver came in and closed the door. He walked over, undid the front button on his lab coat and sat next to Ellie on the couch. "I would like to examine your skin, if it's okay?"

"Sure, go ahead." She sat motionless while he put his hand up to her face.

She wasn't sure if he was feeling for any abnormities or if he was stroking her cheek.

"The epidermis looks quite healthy. Could you open your robe?"

"What?"

"I'd like to see your neck and upper chest."

Ellie slipped her robe down off her shoulders.

Dr. Carver ran his fingers diagonally a few inches above her bra. "Very nice."

Ellie shoved his hand away and closed up her robe. "I don't think this is an appropriate exam."

"Ellie! I assure you, I'm being professional."

Ellie put her palm out and pushed him away. "Please leave."

"I'm sorry if I've upset you. If you don't feel comfortable with me examining you, Dr. Miller can see you instead."

"Yes, please go."

Dr. Carver stood, his face reddening with embarrassment as he buttoned his lab coat. "Ellie, again, I'm sorry if I gave you the wrong impression." He turned and went out the door.

Ellie watched the door, and when she was certain he wasn't coming back, she opened her hand and looked down at Dr. Carver's clip-on employee badge and keycard.

28

SECURITY BREACH

Just to be sure, Ashley had taken her office supplies out of her bottom desk drawer making doubly sure the blue thumb drive memory stick wasn't there. Whoever had broken into her desk hadn't damaged the lock, which meant they either had a spare key to her desk or they knew how to pick the lock. When she was satisfied the flash drive wasn't there, she put everything back in the drawer.

As she had promised, Ashley got up and took the empty coffee pot to fill it up from the water cooler. She came back and poured the water into the coffee maker. She put in the new filter, filled it with coffee grounds, and started the machine.

"Coffee will be in about five minutes," she said, not too loud but enough to get a thank you response from Curtis.

Ashley sat down at her desk. She stared at her blank screen instead of turning on the computer. Why would anyone want to steal the flash drive? From what she could curtail from the data she had updated, there hadn't been any proprietary or confidential information worth stealing. Maybe a coworker had gone in her desk looking for a blank memory stick and took the blue flash drive. But that didn't make any sense, seeing as there was a box of them on her desk next to her monitor.

Whatever the reason, Ashley knew she had to report the theft.

She got up from her desk and went to Dr. Swanson's office.

"Excuse me, but can I speak to you?" Ashley asked, standing in the doorway.

"Sure, come right in, Ashley," Dr. Swanson said, motioning for Ashley to take a seat in the chair in front of her desk.

"If it's all right, could I close the door?"

"Go right ahead."

Ashley shut the door and sat in the chair facing Dr. Swanson.

"Is there something wrong?" Dr. Swanson asked. "I know the preliminary studies can seem mundane."

"It's not that. Someone broke into my desk."

"Oh my God. When?"

"Must have been after I left yesterday."

"Did they take anything?"

"Nothing of mine. Only the USB flash drive I was using to backup the files you've been giving me."

"What about your computer? Could someone have hacked into it?"

"I haven't turned it on yet."

"Well, this is worrisome. Thank you for bringing this to my attention."

"You're welcome." Ashley got up and left the office.

Dr. Swanson picked up her phone. "Jason? Could you come in for a second?"

A minute later, Dr. Carver was standing in the doorway. "What is it?"

"They took the bait."

"So you were right, someone is trying to steal our research. Any idea who?"

"Not yet. How come you're not wearing your badge?"

Dr. Carver looked down at the front pocket on his lab coat. "Shit, I must have dropped it somewhere."

29

MORE TO DIVULGE

Ashley was busting to tell Mitch all about her day when she walked in the front door. "Mitch! *Where* are you?"

"In the backyard," Mitch answered from outside.

Ashley dropped her things on the couch and walked out through the open sliding glass door. "What're you doing?" she asked when she saw Mitch at the picnic table, leaning over Harry's detached arm lying on a sheet of white plastic.

"Quiet, I'm counting," Mitch replied. "Two hundred and one, two hundred and...damn, now I have to start all over."

"You already know how many suction cups there are on an octopus' arm."

"That's textbook. I want to see for myself."

"Where's Dougie?"

"He's in the house, on his pillow."

"I shouldn't have yelled at him," Ashley said, sitting on the bench seat across from her husband.

"Yeah, well, I don't think it was intentional."

"Why's that?"

"You said the bathroom door was closed when you came home yesterday. I got to thinking, what if Harry had managed to slither in and Dougie tried to stop him and the door slammed shut?"

"So you're calling it an accident?"

"It's not like Dougie viciously ripped it off; Harry merely cast off his arm to get free. I doubt he felt a thing."

Ashley called out, "Dougie, come here, boy!"

The Cairn terrier appeared at the open sliding glass door.

Mitch scooted down to the end of the bench. He leaned forward with his elbows on his knees. "Dougie Sanders. It is the decision of this court that you are innocent of said crime and are free to once again get into mischief."

"Did you hear that, Dougie?" Ashley said, clapping her hands. "All is forgiven."

Dougie wagged his tail, bolted across the patio, and leaped onto Ashley's lap. She stroked the back of his neck and looked at Mitch. "So you really were going to turn our bathtub into a fish pond."

"Seemed like a good idea at the time," Mitch said with a shrug.

"How about we call a truce and no more practical jokes?"

"What's the fun in that?"

"Mitch, I'm serious."

"Fine, no more pranks."

"Something strange happened today. Someone broke into my desk at work."

"Are you serious? Please tell me they didn't steal anything out of your purse."

"No, the only thing they got was a flash drive."

"Must have been important."

"Not really," Ashley said.

"Did you report it?"

"I did. There's something else I was meaning to tell you. Remember those three people I told you about who had those terrible accidents?"

"Yeah," Mitch said. "One lost a leg, right?"

"That would be Don Lamont."

"Didn't the other guy get his hand chopped off?"

"His name is Stan McMillan. There was also a girl, Ellie Phelps, she was severely burned by a grease fire." Dougie began to get restless on Ashley's lap so she let him jump down. She leaned in closer like a corporate spy about to divulge a trade secret. "What would you say if I told you it's like those horrible things never happened?"

"I don't understand."

"I saw them. I wasn't supposed to but I did. Lamont has his leg back, McMillan his hand and Ellie Phelps no longer has those ugly burns."

"Ash, that's crazy. How's that even possible?"

"I don't know but I'm curious to find out."

30

SLINKING OUT THE DOOR

It was 3:15 in the morning when Ellie heard the light tapping at her door. She was already dressed in a heavy sweater, jeans, and a pair of sneakers. Everything she had brought to the institute was packed in her travel bag, ready to go.

She got up from the couch, grabbed her bag and went to the door. When she opened it, Don and Stan were standing outside, both dressed and carrying their luggage.

"All set?" Don whispered.

"Yes," Ellie replied in a hushed voice.

"Give me the keycard," Stan said.

Ellie gave Stan the keycard she had pilfered from Dr. Carver.

"Let's go," Don said.

They crept single file toward the glass door.

Outside, a breeze was rustling the trees in the moonlight, casting dark shapes into the dimly lit side lobby.

Stan ran the keycard down the reader. A green light came on and the lock disengaged with a clunk. "If when I open the door, an alarm goes off, run like hell."

He pushed open the door but they didn't hear anything.

"Thank God," Ellie said.

"Doesn't mean there isn't a silent alarm," Don said.

"Don's right. We better hurry!" Stan held the door as Ellie and Don scurried out with their bags. He let the door close on its own and dashed after them down the sidewalk to the corner of the building.

They stopped shy of the parking lot.

The lights were on in the front lobby.

"What if there's a security guard on duty and he's calling the police?" Don said.

"You two stay here while I take a look." Stan crept down the sidewalk and peeked inside the lobby.

A security guard was kicked back in a chair with his feet up on the front counter, reading a magazine.

Stan went back to Ellie and Don. "There was no alarm. There's a 24-hour convenience store a couple of miles down the road; we can use their phone to get a ride."

"What if they come after us?" Ellie said.

"And what if they do? They can't force us to stay," Don said.

"We can worry about that later. Right now, I say we get as far away from this place as we can," Stan said.

They hefted their bags and scurried down the frontage road into the night.

31

RISK ASSESSMENT

"I don't believe it," Dr. Swanson said, standing in the middle of Ellie's empty room. She spun around and lashed out at Dr. Carver. "How could you be so stupid, letting her get your keycard?"

"Don and Stan must have put her up to it."

Dr. Miller sat on the arm of one of the club chairs. "So what do we do?"

"We get them back!" Dr. Swanson snapped.

"And how do we do that?" Dr. Carver asked. "Hire someone to kidnap them?"

"Don't be absurd."

"Jason has a point," Dr. Miller said. "You really think they'll be willing to come back here after running away?"

"They signed a contract for God sake!"

"One I doubt would hold up in a court of law," Dr. Carver said.

"Then we have to find a way to persuade them to return. We can't have them wandering around out there unsupervised."

"If you're so worried, Faye, then *why* the hell did you insist we move ahead with the clinical trials?" Dr. Carver said. "Doreen and I kept telling you it was too soon, not to mention reckless. If you don't agree then maybe you should go back and take another look at those videos."

"So there was one negative outcome."

"Try seven."

"Okay, okay seven," Dr. Swanson finally admitted. "But that was out of two hundred tests. Which for your information is 3.5%, which is far below the standard 5% rejection rate. It was only a fluke."

"We're not dealing with production parts; these are people's lives we're talking about."

"Don't you think I know that?"

Dr. Miller jumped in. "Faye, it doesn't concern you the emulators might be unpredictable?"

"Doreen, I'm not naive. I'm well aware of the risks."

"Well, it appears Don, Stan, and Ellie were not," Dr. Carver said, glaring at Dr. Swanson. "Because we never told them. If they had watched those videos, they would never have consented to the procedures. They have no idea the danger we just put them in."

"Jason's right," Dr. Miller said. "They're ticking time bombs."

32

AUTHORIZED SEARCH

It was nearly lunchtime and Ashley had run out of things to do. She was all caught up with her work and was thinking of asking if it would be okay if she left a couple of hours early so she could run some errands. She hated to be stuck at her desk, twiddling her thumbs, even if she was getting paid pretty good money to do so.

Sean swung by her desk with his coffee mug in hand. "I heard Dr. Swanson is on a rampage."

"Why?" Ashley asked.

"Don't know for certain. Only that Libby overheard her arguing with Dr. Carver."

"And here I was going to ask her if I could leave early."

"I wouldn't if I were you."

"Thanks for the warning."

"Anytime."

"You know, if you need for me to do anything, I'm more than happy to help?"

Sean turned and called Libby over. "Ashley wants to know if you need a hand with anything."

"Not at the moment," Libby said. She glanced over her shoulder to make sure no one was standing behind her. "I heard one of the techs went to make a run out to her car and the security guard searched her purse. Turns out, he's been instructed to search everyone's belongings going in and out of the front lobby."

"He can't do that," Sean said. "That's a violation of our civil rights."

"I bet Dr. Swanson ordered it," Ashley said.

"Why? They never did it before," Sean said, unable to hide the indignation in his voice.

"I told her someone broke into my desk."

"Don't tell me we have an office thief in our midst," Sean grumbled. He looked over the cubicle wall and waved for Curtis to join them.

"Son of a bitch!" Curtis said when Sean relayed the news. "Hey, I catch the bastard going through my desk, I'll stick my stapler up his ass."

"Better not leave anything of value in your desks," Ashley said, giving them all a piece of friendly advice.

"I hate that we can't trust people," Libby said.

Ashley couldn't help but wonder the same thing as Libby, Sean, and Curtis walked away to return to their desks.

33

MACY'S PPD

Don and his wife, Macy, sat in the living room of their apartment.

"Honey you had me worried sick," Macy said, her eyes red from crying.

"I know, and again, I'm sorry," Don replied, doing his best to console her. He knew she was in a fragile state. It was as though she was standing precariously atop a precipice and the slightest wrong word could send her plummeting over the edge.

Don held James on his lap. The clean baby smelled of talcum powder, a marked improvement from when Don had walked in the door and discovered his wailing child in a soiled diaper and desperately in need of a bath.

Macy dabbed the tears from her cheeks with a tissue. She was a blubbering wreck, once again having neglected to take her pills for her postpartum depression.

"Why didn't you call?" This time her voice went up an octave.

"Macy, keep your voice down, you'll wake James."

"Sorry," Macy sobbed and blew her nose.

"I told you, they confiscated our phones as soon as we got there. There was no way for me to get in touch with you." He got up from the sofa and walked over to the front window. Cradling James in one arm, Don parted the curtain so he could look out over the veranda and the parking lot below.

So far, no one had come pounding at the door.

Everything had seemingly gone off without a hitch.

By the time they made it down to the 24-hour convenience store, it was almost daybreak. As none of them had their cell phones, they couldn't call a rideshare service and had to resort to using a pay phone outside the store to summon a taxi.

Luckily, Stan had been smart enough to stash some money in his travel bag and spotted both Don and Ellie the cash they needed to get home. When the cab arrived, they all got in and told the driver where they wanted to be let off. They had decided beforehand it was best they weren't taken directly to their homes but dropped off a block or two away, just in case someone was there waiting to take them back to the institute.

Don had hidden in one of the carports across from his apartment for more than an hour to make sure there wasn't a white van or anyone lurking about before he decided the coast was clear and went up and knocked on the door.

When Macy opened the door, she looked a fright. She had dark circles under her eyes from not getting much sleep because of the baby. Her hair was a mess and she looked like she was wearing the same sweatshirt and shorts when he last saw her.

When he went to kiss her, he almost turned away from her sour breath.

Don stepped away from the window.

He took James into his room and put the sleeping baby in his crib.

Don went into the other bedroom. He took off his shoes, changed into a pair of shorts and walked barefoot back out to the living room.

He stood in front of Macy. "Well, what do you think?"

Macy was in a fog and stared at Don's left leg. "It's much better than the one in the closet. It even looks real."

"That's because it is," Don said. "Check this out." He lifted his right foot up and balanced on his left leg. He put both of his feet on the floor and rose up on his tiptoes and came down on his heels.

"My God," Macy gasped.

"I know, isn't it incredible?"

"It's almost *too* perfect."

"Would you rather I had a knobby knee and hammer toes?" Don said jokingly at first.

"No, no of course not. I don't know what I'm saying."

"I can't believe this," Don said, wishing she would get out of this miserable funk and stop being such a buzz kill. He could feel his temper boiling and knew if he snapped at her, it would only send her further into a downward spiral of depression.

Instead, he said in a soothing voice, "How about I run you a bath while James is down for his nap? What do you say? Believe me, you'll feel much better afterwards."

Macy gave him a weak smile.

"Good," Don said, hoping it would be true.

34

A BIT OF A SHOCK

The sun was just coming up when Ellie arrived home.

Ellie lived in a rental duplex and her unit was in the rear of the property away from the street so she had no idea if anyone had followed her and was camping outside.

Which was partly the reason she had her blinds drawn and the lights out.

She had been sitting in the dark, gathering the nerve for most of the morning, before deciding to scroll down the contacts on her cell phone and call Clark.

A half hour later, Ellie nearly jumped out of her chair when she heard the knock on the door. There was no way of knowing if it was Clark or someone from the institute.

It didn't matter either way.

She'd left the door unlocked.

"Come in," she said.

The handle turned and the door inched open, allowing a sliver of penetrating sunlight into the gloomy room.

"Clark?"

"Ellie, it's me."

"Come in quick and shut the door."

Clark ducked inside and closed the door, plunging the room back into darkness.

"Why are you sitting in the dark?"

Ellie heard him move toward the window to open the blinds. "No, don't!"

"Why not?"

"I don't want you to see me, not just yet," Ellie said, staring at his silhouette across the room.

"But why? You know I don't care about your scars."

"Promise me, you won't freak out?"

"Ellie, what's going on?"

"This is going to be a bit of a shock."

"For heaven's sake, what did they do to you?"

Ellie reached over and turned on the lamp next to her chair.

Clark stepped into the light. He became teary-eyed the second he saw her. He lifted his black-rimmed glasses briefly off the bridge of his nose and rubbed his eyes.

He knelt in front of Ellie.

Clark reached out and squeezed both of her hands. "My God, Ellie! You're beautiful!"

35

HANDSHAKE

Instead of barricading himself inside his home, Stan got in his car and drove to his old job. Stan figured once his boss saw Stan was no longer handicapped, he would reconsider and reinstate Stan back to punch press foreman.

But as he was no longer an employee, Stan was not allowed in the workplace and was asked to sit and wait in the lobby. When a considerable amount of time had passed, Stan became irritated.

"Would you mind calling him again?" Stan asked, balling his right hand into a fist and grinding it into his left palm.

"Everyone is quite busy today as you can imagine, Mr. McMillan," the young receptionist said from behind the front counter.

"I know, but I've been waiting for more than an hour."

"I'm sure Mr. Turner will be out shortly."

But when an additional thirty minutes had gone by, and still no one had come out, Stan got so angry he slammed the arm of the chair with the heel of his right hand.

A weird tingling sensation ran up his arm into his shoulder and momentarily coursed throughout his entire body like an electrical shock.

The veins in the back of his hand bulged and the flesh rippled for a fraction of a second.

"What the hell?" he gasped.

"Stan, what are you doing here?" Leo Turner said, waltzing into the lobby.

Stan stood up and extended his right hand to shake with his old boss.

"Jesus, Stan," Turner said, gawking at Stan's hand. "Did you get some kind of hand transplant?"

"Not exactly," Stan said with a laugh. "Don't worry, it's not from a dead guy."

Turner hesitated before grasping Stan's hand.

They began to shake.

"I wanted to talk to you about getting my old job back."

"I'm afraid that's not possible," Turner said, trying to pull his hand free as Stan continued to pump his arm. "Stan, do you mind?"

"And why's that?" Stan heard a knuckle pop.

"Because we already filled the position. God damn it, let go of my hand," Turner shouted, trying desperately to break free from the handshake.

Stan heard a loud, grinding crack and felt a warm stickiness between his fingers as his vise-like grip crushed the other man's hand. He turned and fled the lobby, leaving his ex-boss down on his knees, screaming.

36

FREE PASS

Ashley turned off her computer and made sure her desk was locked. When she grabbed her purse and stood up, she saw Sean, Libby, and Curtis in their cubicles getting ready to leave. "Oh good, we can all walk out together."

Sean turned to Ashley while he slipped on his coat. "Figured if we're going to get our rights violated, we might as well get it over with."

"Sean! It's no big deal. They're only going to inspect our bags," Libby said.

"Not what I heard," Curtis piped in, stepping out of his cubicle. "Ever have a cavity search?"

"What?"

"Curtis is teasing," Ashley said when she saw the horrified look on Libby's face.

"Am I?" Curtis grinned.

Sean walked out of the lab followed by Libby, Ashley, and Curtis. They went single file down the corridor to the door leading into the lobby. As it was an exit, they weren't required to use a keycard.

Ashley saw a security guard she hadn't seen before, standing behind a table a few feet away from the lobby doors. It was set up like a TSA checkpoint so no one would be allowed to pass through the lobby without being searched. A plastic tray was on the table.

"Get ready to drop your drawers," Curtis said to Sean who was up first.

"Up yours," Sean said over his shoulder.

"Mind opening your briefcase?" the guard asked.

"Sure, whatever you say," Sean said in a sarcastic tone and opened the case.

The guard felt around inside, and when he was satisfied with his inspection, he told Sean he could close it. "Mind emptying your pockets and putting everything in the tray?"

"Really?"

"You heard me," the guard said.

Sean took out his wallet, car keys, a comb, some change and put it all in the tray.

"How about your coat?"

"There's nothing in my—" but then Sean paused when he reached in his side pocket. "Who put this in here?" Sean took out a sealed box of staples.

"You do know the penalty for stealing company property?" the guard said.

"I swear I didn't do it."

"I'm afraid I'm going to have to report this to—"

"It's all right," Curtis said, laughing from the back of the line. "We were just playing a joke."

"Oh yeah?" the guard said. "On who? Me or him?"

"Uh...both?"

"Grab your stuff, you can go," the guard told Sean. "And leave the staples."

Libby walked up to the table and spilled the contents of her purse into the tray.

"Ah, you didn't have to do that," the guard said, using a pencil to separate the items. "You may put it all back in your purse."

Libby scooped everything back into her purse. She pulled out an overly used handkerchief from her coat pocket and showed it to the guard.

He shook his head. "Next."

Ashley was about to put her purse on the table when the lobby doors opened and Dr. Swanson walked in.

The guard turned. "Good afternoon, Dr. Swanson."

"Good afternoon. How is everything going?"

"Fine, ma'am."

Ashley caught Dr. Swanson's eye and gave her a smile. Dr. Swanson leaned in close and whispered to the guard, "She's exempt from any search."

"Right." The guard looked at Ashley. "You may go."

Ashley didn't like being singled out and figured the reason she was getting a free pass was because it was her desk that had been broken into.

Nonetheless, she felt awkward, especially being on the receiving end of the suspicious stares from Sean, Libby, and Curtis.

37

FUGITIVE

Stan jumped in his car and fled the parking lot. He sped down a main street he'd traveled hundreds of times and blew through two stop signs and a red light.

He couldn't get the image of his ex-boss out of his head—Leo Turner sprawled on the floor in pure agony, the red polka dot splashes of blood splattering the floor from his mangled hand.

The young receptionist had been so scared, she screamed.

Instead of slowing down, Stan gunned the engine and raced to his house.

Once inside, Stan ran into his bedroom and pulled a gym bag down from the top shelf in his closet.

He had no idea how much time he had before the incident was reported to the police and they came to arrest him.

It was ironic to think he would be charged for 'violence in the workplace' from a company that had turned its back and wanted nothing to do with him after his accident.

Stan went to his dresser and started pulling out drawers, nearly yanking them off of their tracks. He scooped up folded T-shirts, some underwear, socks, sweat pants and stuffed them into his bag.

He heard tires screech outside.

He zipped up his bag and dashed out of the bedroom. He went into the living room to peek out the window.

Two squad cars had pulled up in front of the house.

One cruiser blocked Stan's car parked in the driveway.

Four uniformed policemen got out.

Suddenly now, he was a fugitive.

Stan raced to the rear of the house and bolted out the back door.

He sprinted across the yard, lobbed his bag into the neighbor's yard.

Stan took a split second to glance over his shoulder to make sure there weren't any guns pointed at him before clambering over the fence.

He snatched his bag up off the ground and ran for his life.

38

GREEN USB

Mitch had dinner waiting when Ashley got home—burgers, curly fries, and strawberry milkshakes—a Sanders' traditional guilty pleasure.

Which meant she didn't have to clean up after Mitch.

Well, at least not in the kitchen.

He'd still left things lying about the house, which she planned to tackle once she had finished her meal.

"So how was your day?" Mitch asked like a charmer sharing pleasantries before taking a big bite out of his hamburger as they sat outside at the back porch picnic table.

"I think I might have created a situation at work," Ashley confessed, nibbling on a curly fry.

"Anything to do with your desk getting broken into?"

"They started a new policy and are searching everyone as they leave work."

"They can do that?"

"Apparently. That's not the half of it," Ashley said, wadding up her wrapper and dropping it into the bag. "I was standing in line with the others when Dr. Swanson came into the lobby and told the guard he didn't have to search my bag."

"She singled you out?"

"You should have seen the looks I got from some of my coworkers."

"So now you're what...the boss' pet?" quipped Mitch.

"Shut up, you moron!" Ashley threw a curly fry at her husband.

"Hey!" Mitch protested. "Stop wasting food! I paid good money for this meal."

"Yeah, right."

"While we're on the subject, could you spot me a twenty for gas?"

"Didn't you get paid yesterday?"

"There was a glitch in payroll."

"Meaning Tony stiffed you."

Tony was Tony Delano who owned his own handyman and home remodeling company. He was a one-man show and whenever he needed some additional help, he would always call Mitch at least a few times a month if business was good.

It was usually enough to cover the rent and some, and Tony paid Mitch cash under the table, so it was a win-win as far as Mitch was concerned, which meant he wasn't tied down to a nine-to-five job and could pursue his passion as a marine biologist.

"Tony would never do that," Mitch said in his best mobster voice. "He's a stand up guy."

"My purse is on the kitchen counter." Ashley slurped her milkshake through a straw while Mitch got up and went inside.

Mitch came out a minute later. "What's this?" He was holding up a green USB flash drive.

"I don't know. Where'd you find it?"

"In your purse."

"What?" Ashley jumped up off the bench. "That's not mine."

"Then how did it get there?"

"Someone must have put it in my purse."

"Why? You don't think someone was trying to get you into trouble?"

"I hope not."

"What if they knew you wouldn't be searched."

"But how would they know that?"

"You tell me. Whoever it is, used you to smuggle it out of the office."

"But why?"

"There's only way to find out." Mitch handed Ashley the USB thumb drive and they went inside.

Ashley perched on the edge of Mitch's desk while he sat in his swivel chair and inserted the memory stick in the side of his laptop.

It took about thirty seconds before a file popped up on Mitch's computer with scores of folders.

"Judging by their titles, they're videos of some lab experiments," Mitch said.

"Open that one," Ashley said, pointing at the screen.

Mitch dragged the cursor over and clicked on the folder.

A frozen image of a workbench came on the screen with a red arrow pointer in the center. Mitch clicked on the prompt and started the video.

Nothing seemed to be happening at first.

Then a person appeared carrying a metal tray and placed it on the workbench. The movie camera recording the video was angled in a way so as not to reveal the person's face. Whether that was intentional, it was difficult to say.

"Is that a starfish?" Ashley said, leaning closer to the screen.

"A giant sea star. A good sized one too. Maybe twenty inches wide." The brown five-armed echinoderm's entire body was covered with small blue rings that looked like skin pustules, as if the aquatic creature was diseased with the pox.

"Is there sound?" Ashley asked.

"No, I think it was shut off."

The person in the video was wearing black rubber gloves and was holding a very sharp carving knife.

"Oh, don't tell me," Mitch said.

The person grabbed one of the starfish's arms and sliced it off.

"Holy crap," Ashley said. "That was a little barbaric."

"Yeah, since it's going to take at least a year before it can regenerate a new arm."

A clear plastic container with brown water was set on the table next to the injured starfish.

"What's that? Brine?"

"Looks like it," Ashley said.

"No, there's something else. I can see them moving in the water. They look like tiny jellyfish."

The starfish was picked up and submerged in the brackish water.

"Look, a time stamp just started," Mitch said, pointing to the digital readout in the lower right hand corner of the screen.

Dougie came over and stood up on the side of the desk.

"Oh, Dougie, I'm so sorry," Ashley said. "We forgot all about feeding you."

"Holy shit!" Mitch shouted.

"What, what is it?" Ashley said.

"Look!"

Ashley turned her direction back to the screen.

The gloved hands were in the process of removing the dripping starfish from the container of water.

The starfish had all five arms.

"That can't be right," Mitch said.

"They used a time lapse camera, so what?" Ashley said.

"Look at the time clock."

Ashley was shocked when she looked at the running time on the digital display in the lower right hand corner of the bottom of the screen. "My God, it took only an hour to grow back its arm!"

39

BABY MONITOR

When Don had first gotten home, he'd been worried if Macy was in any condition to care for James. But then he noticed a marked improvement after she had taken her bath, eaten some scrambled eggs Don had prepared, and taken her medication.

Don sat next to Macy on the couch. He was tempted to turn on the television but decided he'd rather they sat and talked.

"How are you feeling?"

"Like a fog's been lifted."

"Means the pills are kicking in."

Macy turned to Don and said, "So you really had to escape that place?"

"It was either that or become a lab rat."

"Don't you think they're going to want that back?" Macy said, motioning to Don's left leg, outstretched over the other one as he rested the heels of his feet on the coffee table.

"Sorry, no refunds. I'm keeping it."

"I love you," Macy said.

"I love you, too," Don said. He leaned over and kissed her softly on the mouth.

They turned and stared at the baby monitor on the coffee table when they heard James begin to cry.

"I was hoping he'd drop off to sleep after having his bottle," Don said.

"He will. Give him a second," Macy said.

A few moments later, James stopped crying.

"Well, aren't you the baby whisperer," Don said. "It's good to see you're back to your old self."

"It's good to be back," Macy replied and rested her head on his shoulder.

"Tired?"

"Exhausted is more like it."

"Then let's say we call it a night."

"You don't want to stay up, just in case?"

"If they haven't showed up by now, I doubt they'll be coming, at least not tonight." Don grabbed the baby monitor and shoved it in his shorts pocket.

And for the first time in a very long time, Don scooped his wife up in his arms and carried her into the bedroom.

***

Don snapped awake when he heard James bawling in his ear. He saw a red light blinking in the dark. He reached over to turn down the volume on the baby monitor and accidentally knocked it off the nightstand. The sound muffled when the device fell speaker-side down on the carpet.

"Shit, smooth move." He turned over in bed. "Macy? Are you getting up or do you want—"

Macy wasn't in bed. Don figured she must have gone into the other room to quiet James as the baby had stopped crying.

Don rolled over, fluffed up his pillow, and was about to drift off when Macy screamed.

"What the hell? Macy!" Don threw back the covers and lunged out of bed.

The floor went out from under him.

He knocked the lamp off the nightstand and landed face down on the carpet, striking his forehead on the plastic baby monitor.

"God damn it," he cursed. Even though the shade was damaged, the lamp was still plugged in. Don turned on the switch.

He looked down expecting to see his left leg but saw only a stump. "What the hell! Am I losing my mind?" It was as though a burglar had snuck in during the night and stole his leg while he slept. Certainly this was all just a bad dream.

But then Macy screamed again.

"Hang on, I'm coming!" Don grabbed the side of the bed and pulled himself up on one foot. He hopped over to the closet, opened the door and grabbed one of his crutches instead of the prosthetic leg propped in the corner.

Due to the extensive damage from his accident, he'd found wearing the artificial limb to be too painful because of the aggravating bone spurs that continued to grow, which would have required undergoing surgeries every year to have his stump reopened and the jagged end of the bone polished, something he decided he was never going to do and was the main reason he had signed up for the clinical trial.

Before he took a single step with his crutch, he realized Macy was no longer screaming.

"Macy? Honey? Are you all right?"

No response. Even the baby monitor on the floor was quiet.

Don made his way out into the hall. He hobbled toward the baby's room and leaned against the doorjamb.

He gazed into his son's room and saw the crib against one wall in the ambient light, the dresser and changing table on the opposite side.

Don staggered in and held onto the crib railing for support.

He heard a gurgling sound from under the blanket.

Leaning over, he was about to reach down and draw back the child's comforter from the small shape underneath when he heard, "Don! Stop!"

He turned and saw Macy with a horrified look on her face, huddled in a dark corner of the room.

She was clutching the baby in her arms.

Don's flesh crawled.

"If you've got James, then what's in the crib?"

40

HOLY SHIT

Ashley and Mitch had been glued to the computer for most of the evening like a couple of obsessed gamers. Some of the videos had been excruciatingly long, while others were short clips suggesting the experiments in question had been aborted, maybe because they weren't yielding the desired results.

In the lengthier videos, the outcomes had been too unbelievable, causing them to wonder if segments of the footage had been altered in hopes of duping investors.

They had just finished watching a ten-minute video of a tailless green iguana grow back the missing appendage in the same amount of time after being submerged in a brown liquid.

"Again, impossible," Mitch said. "That should have taken at least six months, maybe a year to grow back, no way ten minutes."

"Click on that folder," Ashley said.

The left and right side of the image was letterboxed, which told them the video was being recorded on a cell phone. Whoever was taking it, was walking down a corridor and coming to a stop in front of a door. The person's hand reached down and punched in a series of numbers on the touch pad.

"That was stupid," Mitch said. "They just revealed the access code."

"Maybe they didn't realize their mistake."

Mitch looked at Ashley. "You don't think this is why the USB was planted in your purse?"

"I don't know, could be."

They watched as the door was opened and the camera panned the aquariums along the walls inside the room.

"That's the same room Dr. Swanson brought me into my coworkers have been bugging me about."

"Why, what's in those tanks?"

"Dr. Swanson calls them emulators."

"Never heard of them."

"That's because they're a new species."

The camera zoomed in slowly on the tiny school of jellyfish-like creatures, as they swam back and forth inside the tank like a single entity.

The person taking the video began to place their palm against the glass.

"That looks like a woman's hand," Mitch said.

"Probably Dr. Swanson."

The emulators sensed the presence and smashed up against the glass.

"Holy shit, did you see that?" Mitch shouted.

"That looked like predatory behavior," Ashley said, confirming what her husband was thinking.

"I'll say."

They watched as the person—Ashley had assumed was Dr. Swanson—slowly removed her hand.

"Holy shit!" Mitch yelled.

"You said that already," Ashley said, but then she saw the emulators had formed themselves into what looked like the palm side of the woman's hand.

It was so intricate and detailed in every way Ashley could actually see the whirls in the fingertips.

So it hadn't been an illusion that day when she put her finger up to the glass.

"Holy shit is right!"

41

BURNER PHONE

So far Stan had been able to elude the police.

He was thankful it was nightfall by the time he got downtown even though he wasn't too thrilled walking down the sidewalk under the glowing streetlights. He hoped he didn't look too conspicuous as he tried to keep in step with pedestrians out for an evening of shopping, or perhaps wanting to grab a bite of dinner before catching a movie.

When he got too close to a woman, almost bumping into her, she gave him a dirty look and snarled, "Excuse me!"

But instead of saying he was sorry, Stan turned and entered a liquor store.

He went directly up to the wrinkled-faced, gray-haired old man standing behind the glass counter in front of a wall stretching to the ceiling with hundreds of bottles on the shelves.

Stan tapped the glass top on the display case. "I'll take that one."

The clerk unlocked the back of the case and took out a small box with a picture of a flip phone.

"How much?" Stan asked.

"With tax, thirty bucks."

"I'll take it," Stan replied and opened the box. He was about to take the cell phone out of the packaging when the clerk stopped him by saying, "You know you're going to have to charge that thing."

"Jesus, I was hoping I could use it right away."

"I do have a burner phone I could sell you. All ready to go with plenty of minutes."

"Yeah, how much?"

"A hundred bucks."

"What? That's highway robbery."

"You want it or not?"

Stan could tell the man knew he was desperate. He knew it wouldn't do any good to barter with the old coot. "Okay, give me the phone."

The old man reached down and came back up with a mobile phone with a scratched case and cracked screen. "Don't worry, it works."

Stan took five twenties out of his wallet, threw the bills on the counter, and snatched up the phone. He went back out, and found a bench where he could sit. He opened his wallet, took out Dr. Swanson's business card and made the call.

Dr. Swanson answered on the second ring. "Hello?"

"It's Stan McMillan."

"Stan, my God, I was getting worried. Are Ellie and Don with you?"

"No. You've got to help me."

"I will. But first you need to return to the institute."

"You don't understand. I'm in big trouble. The police are after me."

"What did you do?"

Stan glanced across the street and saw a police car cruising in the traffic. "I can't talk right now. I have to go. Can you pick me up?"

"Yes, of course. Where are you?"

"I'll be at the market on Fifth and Rocklin."

"Give me fifteen minutes."

"Just hurry."

42

SEEING DOUBLE

"I'm turning on the light," Don insisted.

"No! Leave it off!" Macy said, still holding the baby and huddled in the dark corner of the room.

"Macy, you're being ridiculous." Don would have hobbled over to the switch if it weren't for the panic in her voice.

"I'm scared."

"Scared of what? Standing in the dark?" he said facetiously.

"You don't get it!"

"Get what?"

"I may have grabbed the wrong one."

Don turned his attention to the shape moving under the baby blanket inside the crib. "What are you saying?"

"There were two of them when I came into the room."

"Two what?"

"God damn it, Don! Our baby! There were two of them."

"Bullshit! That's it!" Don used his crutch to hop over and turned on the light switch by the bedroom door.

As soon as the ceiling light came on, Macy gasped, "Don, your leg! What happened to your leg?"

"Maybe a better question would be 'Where the hell did it go?'" Don glanced down at the carpet and saw a wet trail leading into the room from the hallway to the crib.

He looked over at Macy. She stood frozen with her eyes shut like she was afraid to open them and look down at the bundle in her arms.

Don could see the top of the tiny pink head sticking out. "Macy? It's okay. Open your eyes."

"Not until you tell me what's in the crib. Is it our son or not?"

Don could see she was freaking out. There was only one way to be sure. He went back over to the crib. He hesitated for a moment before reaching down and lifting off the blanket.

His first reaction was that it was indeed James but he didn't want to say anything out loud for fear he might be wrong and Macy would drop whatever was in her arms.

"Well? Is it?" Macy persisted.

"Just give me a second." Don knew he would be a poor excuse for a father as he looked at the sleeping baby if he couldn't recognize his own son but the resemblance was uncanny right down to the cherub face and the button nose.

Somehow, the disposable diaper had come off and had been kicked to the side leaving the baby naked.

"Is your James wearing a diaper?" Don asked, knowing how absurd the question sounded.

"No. I can feel his bare butt."

"That's no help," Don replied. The only thing he could conclude with some degree of certainty was that the baby had ten fingers, ten toes and was circumcised just like James. "The only way to be sure is for you to bring *him*"—emphasizing the word *him* when he almost said *it*—"over here so we can compare."

"I can't. You come and get him."

"Macy, give me a break. I'm on crutches."

"Okay but I'm handing him off once I get to the crib."

Don leaned against the railing and put out his hands. "I'm ready."

Macy looked straight ahead, not once looking at what she was carrying, and crossed the room, handing Don the sleeping baby.

Don took the baby and placed it in the crib alongside the other fast asleep baby. It was like he was seeing double.

"My God, they're identical," Macy said, finally getting the nerve to look inside the crib. "But how is this possible?"

"I'll tell you how it happened," Don said with a chuckle. "Somehow my leg decided to crawl out of bed, came in here and miraculously turn into a clone of our son. The question is: which one is the real James?"

43

SLIGHT OF HAND

Instead of standing outside to wait for Dr. Swanson, Stan decided it would be wiser if he went inside the Asian market, which was roughly the size of a basketball court in a high school gymnasium with two checkout stands and a dozen aisles, the meat, poultry, fish and produce sections at the rear of the store.

Stan hoped he didn't look too conspicuous being that most of the customers were Asian and he was the only one wandering the aisles carrying a gym bag instead of a shopping basket.

He stood in the back where he had a clear view down one of the aisles and could see everyone coming into the store.

This was the first time Stan had ever been inside this particular store and was surprised how different it was from where he normally shopped.

Instead of packaged chicken, he saw scores of plucked poultry hanging from hooks behind the butcher's counter. Live fish, crabs and lobsters were crowded separately for customers to choose from inside half a dozen large aquariums.

The automatic doors slid open.

Dr. Swanson came in and immediately started scanning the store, looking for Stan.

He gave her a short wave to get her attention and she hurried up the aisle.

"Stan, thank God you came to your senses," Dr. Swanson said. "I really must get you back to the institute."

"Do you have any idea what I've done?" Stan said.

"We can talk about that later, but first we need—"

"I assaulted my boss. For all I know, I may have killed him."

"What are you talking about?"

"We were in the middle of a handshake when I crushed the man's hand." Stan balled his right hand into a fist and wielded it in her face. "It was like I had no control of this thing. What the hell did you do to me?"

"Stan, keep your voice down."

Unbeknownst to Stan, his rant had drawn the attention from the other customers.

"We really need to get you out of here," Dr. Swanson said.

But as they headed down the aisle, the front entrance door opened, and in stepped a uniformed police officer. He glanced at his cell phone and began looking around at the people in the store. It wasn't until he spotted Stan that he slipped the phone in his trouser pocket and placed his hand on his holstered gun.

"Ah shit," Stan swore under his breath.

"You sir, are you Stan McMillan?" the officer called out.

"Yes."

"Drop the bag and put your hands on your head," the officer ordered. "Don't make me have to draw my weapon."

"Officer, if I may speak," Dr. Swanson said.

"Who are you?"

"My name is Faye Swanson. I'm Mr. McMillan's doctor."

"What kind of doctor?"

"I'm a biomedical engineer. Mr. McMillan is under my care."

"I'm sorry, but he's coming with me and is under arrest for assault." The officer walked up to Stan. "Now turn around."

Stan did what he was told.

The officer grabbed Stan's left hand first and brought his arm around his back and then did the same with his right hand, putting him in handcuffs.

"Do they have to be so tight?" Stan said, feeling the manacles cutting into his wrists.

"Please, Officer," Dr. Swanson said, standing in front of the police officer and blocking him from going down the aisle.

"Lady, unless you want to join him, I suggest you move out of my way," the officer said, dragging Stan by the arm.

"But you don't understand."

"I'm not going to tell you again."

Stan felt the handcuffs suddenly give way and he was able to raise his arms out in front of him. His left hand was still in the handcuffs but his right was free because he no longer had a right hand.

"How the hell did you break out of those?" the officer said, gawking at Stan's stump. "Were you wearing a rubber hand?"

Stan heard a commotion, and when he turned, he saw cardboard boxes of noodles toppling off the shelves.

"What in the holy hell is that?" the officer shouted and drew his gun.

Stan caught a fleeting glimpse of the thing that had once been his hand claw its way up and launch itself into the next aisle causing a woman to scream from the other side.

44

JEALOUS BOYFRIEND

When Clark tried to kiss her, Ellie stopped him because she wasn't sure if she was ready. Which is why she was sitting in the chair while Clark had moved over to the sofa on the other side of the coffee table.

"I don't understand," Clark said. "I thought you liked me."

"I do, very much. I'm just not sure if it's safe for us to get intimate."

"Why, is that what the doctors told you after you had the cosmetic surgery?"

"I never had surgery. To tell you the truth, I have no idea how they did it. I remember being in a bathing suit and lying in a glass tub. Then I was put under. When I woke up, I was normal again."

"But how did they remove all your scar tissue?" A horrified look came over Clark's face. "Oh my God, Ellie, don't tell me they removed skin from other parts of your body so they could do a skin graft on your face."

"No, Clark. They didn't take skin off of my butt."

"I wouldn't care even if they did." Clark moved off the couch and sat on the edge of the coffee table so he could be closer to Ellie.

"Which would mean if we were to make out, you would be literally kissing my ass."

Clark let out a laugh. "I'm good with it if you are."

"To be honest I did miss you," Ellie said.

Clark moved to the sofa and patted the cushion next to him. "And I—"

They both jumped when they heard a loud pounding at the front door.

"Who's that?" Clark said, glancing at the clock. "It's after eight."

"Jesus, please don't tell me it's someone from the institute to take me back."

"No one's forcing you to go back," Clark said, jumping up from the sofa. "Not as long as I'm here." He marched over to the front door.

"Clark, don't answer the door. Maybe they'll think I'm not here and go away."

"I'm sure they've seen the light on. No, let me handle this." Clark opened the front door and was met with a fist to the face. He stumbled backward and fell flat on the floor.

Ray stormed in and slammed the door. He looked down at Clark and turned to Ellie. "You dumped me for this guy?"

"Ray, what are you doing here? Get out! Leave us alone!" Ellie pleaded.

"Not until I'm through with this clown." Ray walked over, grabbed the front of Clark's shirt and lifted him a few inches off of the floor so he could punch Clark in the jaw.

"You bastard!" Ellie screamed, running at Ray and shoving him off balance.

He caught himself and grabbed Ellie by the arm.

"You're hurting me! Let go!" Ellie yelled, struggling to get free.

"Hey, what the hell?" Ray said, staring at Ellie's face. "I thought you got all burned up?" He glanced down at Clark and looked back into Ellie's eyes. "Come on, you know you missed me. How about giving Ray a little kiss?"

"I'd rather die first." Even though Ellie was frightened, she could feel a rage building up inside her like a boiling teakettle about to blow out steam.

"Ellie?" Clark muttered, trying to roll over on the floor, shaken from the punch.

"Ray! I'm warning you! Get your hands off of me!"

Ray yanked her towards him and kissed her firmly on the mouth.

Ellie felt her face flush the same instance Ray made a panicked moaning sound.

Able to pull her head back, Ellie took one look at Ray and screamed because for a split second he looked exactly like her before his eyelids, nostrils, and lips sealed shut like they had been glued together and his face turned dark blue.

He clawed at his mouth, trying to rip his lips apart, unable to breathe. He fell to his knees and then onto his side, twitching on the floor.

A minute later, he was dead.

Clark managed to sit up. He looked over at Ray. "What happened? Is that your jealous boyfriend? I thought you two broke up."

"We did."

Clark looked up at Ellie. "Oh my God, Ellie. Your face!"

Ellie gazed into a mirror hanging on the wall.

She looked her normal self except for the dark rings of scar tissue on both her eyes and patches of damaged skin under her nose and around her mouth.

45

ADORABLE TWINS

Dr. Miller went up the cement stairs to the second terrace and walked briskly down the landing and knocked on the Lamont's apartment door.

"Thank God, you came," Don said, opening the door a crack.

"I must say, I'm surprised you called," Dr. Miller said. "I thought you, Stan and Ellie would be long gone by now."

Don opened the door wide enough for Dr. Miller to step through before he closed it behind her.

Right off, Dr. Miller noticed Don was using a crutch. "Where's your leg?"

"It's over there on the couch. At least I think it is."

Dr. Miller saw two babies lying next to each other beside a haggard young woman.

"This is my wife, Macy," Don said, making the introductions. "Macy, this is Dr. Miller from the institute."

"Hi," Macy said.

"Pleased to meet you. I see you have two adorable twins," Dr. Miller said, gazing at the two babies fast asleep on the couch. "But I don't see your leg."

"That's just it," Don said. "We only have one son."

"You're going to think we're terrible parents," Macy said, sitting sideways on the couch so she could look down at the identical babies. "But we can't tell our son from the imposter which we think was Don's leg."

"Certainly there must be a way to tell them apart," Don said, hopping over to a recliner chair and sitting down.

"There might be, but first tell me what happened."

"I woke up, realized my leg was gone, and when Macy went into James' room, there were two of them."

"Doctor, we're desperate here," Macy pleaded. "Can you help us?"

"Well, let me see," Dr. Miller said, walking over to the couch.

As the babies were wearing only diapers, Dr. Miller took a couple of minutes to examine each of their bodies, looking for any inconsistencies only to conclude they were exactly the same in every way.

"Well?" Macy said.

"I have to say I can't tell the difference."

"Then there's nothing you can do?"

"I didn't say that," Dr. Miller said and sat down on a chair next to Don. "But you might not like what I am about to suggest."

"Why?" Macy asked. "You're not going to hurt my baby, are you?"

"First of all, I need to explain how we were able to give Don his new leg before I can tell you what's going on here," Dr. Miller said.

"I've been meaning to ask you about that," Don said. "How the hell did you do it?"

"We replicated your leg with a regenerative organism we call emulators. Actually your leg is made up of thousands of them working in unison." Dr. Miller glanced at the babies. "As you can see, they have the ability to mimic any living thing they choose."

"And who created these things?" Don said. "Dr. Swanson?"

"As well as Dr. Carver and myself. We tried to convince Dr. Swanson that we thought it was much too soon to start any human clinical trials. We warned her about the risks but she wouldn't listen."

"What kind of risks?" Macy asked.

"Emulators are, for lack of a better word, a hodgepodge of marine animals that have one thing in common, they can regenerate and duplicate any living thing they come in contact with. But they can be unpredictable. But there's a bigger concern."

"And what's that?" Don asked.

"Like all living creatures, no matter how small, they have a defense mechanism when they are threatened. As an example, Dr. Swanson insisted we use sea cucumbers as part of the emulators' DNA because they use blastulation to repair injured cells. Only problem is they also emit a poisonous toxin whenever they feel they are under attack."

"So, what are you saying?" Macy said.

"We're going to have to run a test as the emulator will lash out in order to protect itself."

"So what do we do?" asked Don. "Stick the bottoms of their feet with a pin?"

"I don't think a pin prick would do it. I know it sounds barbaric, but do you have any matches?"

"Absolutely not!" Macy snapped. "I'm not letting you hurt my baby."

"Macy, it's the only way, I assure you. I promise I'm not going to burn them, only apply some heat so they will react."

"Honey, let Dr. Miller do her test. It's the only way we're going to know which one is James," Don said.

"Okay, I'll get them," Macy said reluctantly and went into the kitchen. She came back and handed a box of stick matches to Dr. Miller.

"Before we start, do you have a container, an ice chest perhaps?" Dr. Miller asked. "And some duct tape."

"Yes, in the closet," Don said.

"Macy, could you get it please."

"Sure." Macy went into the hall closet and brought out a blue ice chest and a roll of duct tape.

"I want you to hold the lid open. If what I think is about to happen, I want you to be ready to close it quick and seal it with the duct tape." Dr. Miller looked at Macy. "Are you up for this?"

"I am," Macy replied, positioning the open ice chest in front of the couch.

"What should I do?" Don asked.

"You might want to sit on the other side of the couch and have your crutch ready in case it decides to go your way."

Macy made sure the sleeping babies were propped upright with their bare feet pointed at Dr. Miller.

"Here goes nothing," Dr. Miller said, dragging the head of a match across the striker.

46

STORE WIDE PANIC

"Stay where you are and don't move!" ordered the police officer. He gave Dr. Swanson a glaring look. "That goes for you too, lady. I'm not through with you just yet." He turned and crept around the aisle with his gun in both hands.

Stan could hear people screaming and running about the store, some even fleeing out the front entrance. He looked at Dr. Swanson. "Screw this, we need to get out of here."

"Not until I see what's happening," Dr. Swanson said.

Before he could protest she was already heading to the rear of the market. "Jesus," he muttered and followed her, as he knew she was his only way out of this mess.

When he caught up to Dr. Swanson, they both stood and watched the bedlam.

"Everyone get out!" the police officer yelled, training his gun on the glass display counter in the butcher's section. Workers in white aprons scrambled to get out of the way as the officer went through a swinging rubber door.

"Oh my God, there it is," Dr. Swanson said, pointing at one of the fish tanks.

Stan saw something inside the tank crawling over the backs of the crabs. It was shaped like Stan's hand but looked more like a jellyfish pulling itself along by its tentacles rather than fingers. Each time it touched one of the crustaceans, the thing would shape shift in the blink of an eye into a hard-shell crab and then revert back in a split second to its gelatin state as it moved on to the next crustacean.

The officer saw the creature in the tank and yelled, "Get out of the way!" He fired a single shot into the tank. The bullet hole shattered the glass and gallons of water spilled out onto the floor, freeing the crabs to scuttle in all directions.

"We need to leave before more cops show up," Stan said.

"Not yet," Dr. Swanson replied.

"Are you listening to me? Let's get out of here while we still can while he's distracted trying to kill that thing."

Dr. Swanson turned to Stan. "That's just it. I don't think he can kill it."

"What do you mean?"

"I mean if he does shoot it and it dies, its decaying body will just regenerate new polyps and create more emulators."

Stan heard another gunshot. He saw the officer making his way over to the bakery section behind a glass display case of almond cookies and cakes. Stan turned and saw two more police officers charge into the store. They must have heard the gunshot from outside because they had their guns drawn.

Dr. Swanson stepped in front of Stan so the officers wouldn't see him and yelled, "He's back there!"

The officers rushed past and ran behind the counter.

"I think it went in the freezer," said the officer that had tried to arrest Stan.

"What the hell is it?" said one of the responding officers.

"Shit, I don't know."

Dr. Swanson grabbed Stan's arm and pointed at the emulator eluding the police officers and scampering into the fish section. It crawled up onto a large cutting block and lay next to a 16-inch salmon waiting to be gutted and filleted.

"It's now or never."

Before Stan could object, Dr. Swanson snuck behind the counter. Stan knew if he tried to run, the cops would see him trying to escape, so he kept low and followed Dr. Swanson.

The emulator had already taken on the form of the salmon, which would have been the perfect disguise, if Dr. Swanson hadn't seen the transformation. She scooped the replica off of the cutting board and into a trash bin lined with a black heavy-duty plastic bag. She fastened the drawstrings and sealed up the bag. "Here, you carry it," she whispered and handed Stan the bag.

They snuck into the store's warehouse and went out through the back to find Dr. Swanson's car.

47

TURNING IN

It was getting late so Mitch and Ashley decided it was time to turn in. They had been up most of the evening viewing one video clip after another until they had gotten bleary-eyed and called it quits.

Ashley let Dougie out so he could do his business before they secured the house for the night. She turned off the lights and followed the Cairn terrier into the bedroom.

Dougie wasted no time and jumped up on the foot of the bed.

Mitch hit the bathroom first and began brushing his teeth with the door open. He spat and rinsed, then glanced out at Ashley, as she was turning down the bed. "Still doesn't explain why someone put that flash drive in your purse."

Ashley stopped what she was doing and sat on the edge of the bed to look at her husband. "Isn't it obvious? Someone's trying to steal the institute's research."

"Well, yeah, I get that," Mitch said, coming over and sitting beside Ashley. "But why involve you?"

"I don't know because I'm the new kid on the block? Maybe they thought I wouldn't discover it and were planning to lift it from my purse later."

"Yeah, that would make sense," Mitch said, scratching his chin. "I was surprised I found it buried under all of your junk. You should really think about cleaning out your purse once in awhile."

"Really, you're giving me cleaning tips?"

"Just saying."

"Do you believe this guy?" Ashley said to Dougie curled up at the end of the bed.

"We should hit it," Mitch said.

Ashley ducked in the bathroom for a minute and came back out. She got into bed on her side and switched off the lamp on her nightstand.

"I wonder what the punishment is for stealing company secrets?" Mitch said, staring up at the ceiling.

"What, now we're corporate spies?"

"Kind of feels that way," Mitch said.

"Where did you hide the flash drive?"

"Some place where no one will ever find it, trust me."

48

EENY MEENY MINY MOE

Dr. Miller was indecisive as she held the burning matchstick, contemplating which baby she should test first. They both looked so innocent and sweet, certainly not a threat to anyone. She waited too long and the flame almost burned her fingers before she shook it out. "This is harder than I thought."

"Maybe there's another way," Don said, leaning forward on the couch.

"What if we pinch one?" Macy said. "It might hurt at first but it shouldn't leave a mark."

"That's a good idea," Don agreed.

"All right," Dr. Miller said.

"Probably best if you do it. We don't want our son thinking Macy and I enjoy hurting him."

"Good point." Dr. Miller put the box of matches on the floor. She looked at the baby on the left, then the one on the right. "It's hard to decide."

"Then go eeny, meeny, miny, moe," Don said.

"Not what I would call a scientific approach."

"If it will make it any easier on you, start with the one on your left."

"Okay, here goes." Dr. Miller started the nursery rhyme going from left to right and counting off with every syllable. "Eeny, meeny, miny, moe, catch a baby by the toe, if he hollers, let him go, eeny...meeny...miny..."

Don and Macy watched with anticipation as Dr. Miller shouted, "MOE," and pinched the baby on the right, hard on his left leg.

The baby woke up and screamed bloody murder.

"Oh thank God," Macy said, rushing over to scoop up her son.

"I still need your help."

"Sorry, Dr. Miller," Macy said, "but this is your problem now, not ours."

"How do you know you're holding the real James?" Dr. Miller asked.

Macy looked at James' face. "Because those are real tears he's crying."

Dr. Miller grabbed the box off the floor. She took out a stick match, lit it, and touched the bottom of the baby's foot, sitting on the couch.

The baby's head and body immediately dissolved into a gelatin blob and its arms and legs stretched out into flailing tentacles. It lunged itself off the couch but Dr. Miller was ready with the open ice chest. As soon as the thing slammed into the lid, Dr. Miller closed it and sealed the emulator inside with bands of duct tape.

Don stood awestruck. "You mean that thing was attached to me?"

"Not anymore," Dr. Miller said, picking up the ice chest by the handles and heading for the door.

49

THE BODY

Ellie and Clark had been standing over Ray's dead body for what seemed forever deciding what they should do.

"Sure you don't want to call the police?" Clark said.

"And tell them what? My psycho boyfriend," Ellie paused, "sorry, my ex-boyfriend..."

"I was hoping you were going to say that," Clark said with a smile.

Ellie continued by saying, "Broke in, cold cocked you and when he came at me, I somehow gave him the kiss of death."

"I'd prefer if you said he *sucker punched* or *blindsided* me."

"Clark! I'm serious," Ellie said.

"Sorry. Maybe you have some kind of ability?"

"What, like a super power?"

"No, you're right, that wouldn't do. Oh, I know. How about we tell them you were a victim of some diabolical experiment? Which probably isn't far from the truth."

"By that you mean botched experiment. Look at me, I'm ugly again."

"No, you're not. It just wasn't quite the success you had hoped for."

"What, now I'm Bride of Frankenstein?"

"You know, I always thought Elsa Lanchester was too hot to be a monster."

"Yeah, you would."

"What, you don't think so?" Clark said, looking at Ellie.

"Clark, can you please be serious for just one second?" Ellie said.

"Again, sorry." Clark returned his attention back to Ray's dead body. "Jesus, that's royally messed up."

Ray's facial features were rubbed out as though a sketch artist had erased Ray's eyes, nose, and mouth.

"That was some kiss," Clark said.

"Shut up," Ellie snapped.

Clark looked at Ellie. He hesitated for a moment before putting his hands on both her shoulders. "I have a theory."

"Yeah, and what's that?"

"This is going to sound cuckoo. But I think those doctors used an unstable mutation to rejuvenate your skin. When Ray forced himself on you, and you felt threatened, the mutation expelled itself from your body on to his, killing him."

"You've been watching too many science fiction movies."

"No, really," Clark said. "They call it transference."

"Now you're making it up."

Clark shook his head and smiled. "I know you're not going to believe me, but I still think you're beautiful."

"No, I'm not. I'm hideous."

"Not from where I'm standing."

"Prove it!"

Clark leaned in and kissed her passionately on the lips. "See," he said when their lips parted, "I didn't even have to close my eyes."

"I closed mine," Ellie said with a wry grin.

"So what are you saying? Girls don't make passes at guys who wear glasses?"

Ellie looked down at Ray's body. "He's starting to freak me out."

"Where do you keep your linen?"

"In the cabinet there," Ellie pointed.

Clark went over, opened the door and took out a folded sheet. He shook out the sheet and draped it over the body. "There, out of sight, out of mind."

"For now. We can't just leave him there on the floor."

"We could carry him out, put him in his car."

The thought of touching him gave Ellie the creeps. "No, we better not."

"Then what do you want to do?"

"What I should have done in the first place."

50

UNKNOWN CALLER

Dr. Carver had tried reaching Dr. Swanson and Dr. Miller on their cell phones but each time he was directed to their voicemail. He texted them both and got the same result. Normally they would have responded immediately. Now it was like they were either purposely ignoring his messages or they had turned their phones off.

Somehow, he knew it had something to do with the patients that had fled the facility.

His first reaction was there had been medical emergencies and both Dr. Swanson and Dr. Miller had been summoned. Which didn't explain why he hadn't been notified.

Unless it had to do with Ellie Phelps' accusation that he had attempted to grope her while he gave her a physical exam that kept Stan and Don from trusting Dr. Carver and trying to contact him.

Which now he knew was utter bullshit as Ellie had only made a scene when he touched her face so she could snag his keycard badge without him being aware. He later learned the truth after reviewing the printout history of the person that exited the side lobby and Dr. Carver saw only his name and badge number at that weird hour of the morning.

It wasn't typical for him to be in his office so late as it was nearly ten in the evening.

He got up from his desk, raised his arms up over his head and stretched. When he worked the muscles in his upper back to get the kinks out he heard his spine pop back into alignment.

Dr. Carver stepped out into the hall.

He looked to his left and then to the right.

The ends of the corridors were dark, the only light shining into the hall coming from the reading lamp on his desk.

He figured besides the security guard in the front lobby, he was the only one left in the building and didn't see any point in sticking around. If Dr. Swanson or Dr. Miller couldn't give him the courtesy of keeping him informed in what was going on, to hell with them. He'd be sure to give them both a piece of his mind, come tomorrow morning.

He went back into his office and stood in front of the large aquarium.

As it was difficult to see inside the tank with the bulb from his reading lamp on his desk reflecting on the front pane of the tank, he reached up and switched on the tubular light fixture recessed in the aquarium's cover. A subtle light shone down through the water like the penetrating rays of the sun from a blue sky.

Dr. Carver grabbed a pointer stick. He slid back the lid slightly and inserted the stick into the water. He used the tip and began poking about the gravel on the bottom of the tank.

The blue-ring octopus jetted across the tank the moment it got prodded by the stick. Its entire body turned yellow and lit up with 50 flashing blue rings, operating much like light reflectors set out to alert motorists of impending roadwork.

Only this warning system was deadly.

The blue-green light was triggered by dark pigmented chromatophores, which enabled the octopus to change its texture and color by contracting and relaxing its muscles thus altering its appearance whenever it felt threatened.

In other words: *Leave me the hell alone or I will kill you!*

"Ah, there you are," Dr. Carver said with a grin. He knew he was tempting fate every time he interacted with the deadly sea creature.

Sometimes when he pulled out the pointer stick there would be a slight residue from the octopus' venom.

Luckily, for the octopus it was immune to its own venom, which was 10,000 times deadlier than arsenic, but as it had to store such a high concentration of poison in its body, Nature decided there would have to be a tradeoff so the blue-ring lost the ability to jet out black ink as a defense mechanism.

It wasn't as though Dr. Carver had a death wish whenever he was with Blueblood.

Call it more of an adrenaline rush.

Or maybe it was Dr. Carver just being defiant. When he had first brought the octopus to the institute, Dr. Swanson had voiced her concern about his insistence in keeping such a dangerous animal in his office. But then they came to terms, agreeing there was really no difference from Dr. Carver having a similar species in his office than what they had floating around in the laboratories.

"Night, Blueblood. I'll feed you in the morning." Dr. Carver switched off the aquarium's light and made sure the cover was sealed properly. He was about to walk out of his office when his cell phone rang.

He looked at the screen and saw UNKNOWN CALLER on the display. "Hello?"

"Dr. Carver?"

"Yes."

"It's Ellie."

"I've been worried about you," Dr. Carver said, thinking it was about time someone contacted him. "Are you all right?"

"No, I'm not. I need you to come over to my place right away."

"Sure, I'll be right there."

"And please hurry. Something terrible has happened."

51

MOTION DETECTORS

Mitch woke up to an outdoor spotlight shining in his face through the bedroom window curtains. He elbowed Ashley lightly in the ribs. "Ash, wake up."

"Hey, knock it off."

"They're here."

"Who's here?"

"Those damn raccoons."

"So, go back to sleep."

"No way, not this time." Mitch jumped out of bed and went over to the closet. He opened the door and pulled out a spear gun.

Ashley sat up in bed. "What are you doing? Don't even think about it."

"I'm not going to shoot them, just scare them away."

"Not with that you're not. Put it back, this isn't an episode of *Sea Hunt*."

"I'm going out there anyway." Mitch tossed the spear gun back in the closet and closed the door. "Dougie, ready to chase off some rustlers?"

The Cairn terrier perked up his ears and sprang off the bed.

"Good to see Dougie has my back."

"Just promise you won't hurt them," Ashley said and fell back into bed.

"You do know raccoons can be pretty vicious when they're in a pack."

"Yeah, yeah." Ashley waved at him to go away and rolled over in bed.

Mitch decided not to turn on the lights as he and Dougie crept through the house to the sliding glass door. He peeked outside and saw the pond area brightly illuminated by the spotlights but didn't see any raccoons. Just because they weren't out in plain sight didn't mean they weren't out there.

He reached down to raise the lever to unlock the sliding glass door and was surprised to discover it was already unlocked. Mitch turned and called out, "Ash, did we forget to lock the back door?"

"Just come back to bed," was Ashley's reply.

"No, seriously. It's unlocked!"

"I don't know. Maybe."

Mitch looked down at Dougie waiting patiently by the door. "So much for home security, eh boy?" Mitch grabbed the handle and slid open the door.

Dougie bolted outside.

"Go get 'em, boy!"

While Mitch waited for Dougie to make his sweep of the backyard, he took a closer look at the doorjamb's metal frame from the outside. The track was dented like someone had tried to pry the door open.

"Ash! You better get out here!"

A few seconds later, Ashley flicked on the hall light and came stomping down the hall. She tied the sash on her bathrobe and shot Mitch one of her *'this better be good'* looks. "What?"

"I think someone tried to break in. I never noticed this before, so it must have just happened tonight."

"Are you serious?"

"Take a look for yourself. Looks like they tried using a screwdriver or a tire iron to get in."

Ashley walked over and examined the doorjamb. "You're right. Strange, I haven't heard of any burglaries being reported in the neighborhood. It's not like we have anything worth stealing."

"What about my research?" Mitch said.

"Yeah, well, there is that." Ashley looked at Mitch. "Oh my God, Mitch. What if they were after the flash drive?"

"What's keeping Dougie?" Mitch said. "He should be back by now."

Dougie began barking like crazy.

Mitch saw the silhouette of a person race along the fence line and dart out the side gate.

Dougie strutted back to Mitch and Ashley, having chased the intruder away.

"You're such the big boy," Ashley said, using her husky voice.

"Good job, Dougie." Mitch bent down and gave the pooch a pat on the head.

"Listen," Ashley said. A car engine had started somewhere on the street; a second later the vehicle sped away.

"They won't be coming back," Mitch said. "At least not tonight." He waited until Ashley and Dougie were inside before locking the sliding glass door.

"Still doesn't mean I'll be able to sleep," Ashley said as they padded barefoot down the hallway after Dougie.

Five minutes later, Ashley was snoring on her back, sawing down a national forest while Mitch lay awake with the spear gun on the floor beside him and stared at the window, waiting for the motion detectors to trigger the backyard spotlights; much like a rancher sitting in wait for a nighttime predator to attack his herd.

52

WHAT ABOUT RAY?

Dr. Carver found Ellie Phelp's duplex with no problem and parked in the driveway behind a yellow Mustang. He got out of his car, went around to the rear unit and knocked on the door.

A nerdy-looking young man with horn-rimmed glasses answered. "Are you Dr. Carver?"

"In the flesh. And you are?"

"I'm Clark Baxter."

"I take it you're Ellie's boyfriend?"

"Yeah, that's right," Clark beamed.

"Is that your yellow Mustang in the driveway?"

"No, mine's parked in the street."

"Clark! Let Dr. Carver in," Ellie said, standing in the dark living room.

Dr. Carver walked in and gazed about the room, wondering why all the lights had been turned off except for a lamp on an end table next to an armchair. "What, are you two living in a cave? How about we turn on some lights?"

"I will, but first let me say how sorry I am about tricking you," Ellie said. "I feel real bad. I hope I didn't get you into trouble."

"No, not at all," Dr. Carver lied. "But if it will make you feel any better, I know Stan and Don put you up to it," he said, figuring the sooner he let her off the hook the better.

Ellie stepped into the light.

Dr. Carver saw the partial scarring on her face. He approached Ellie to take a closer look. "I hope your immune system isn't rejecting the treatment."

"I don't think that's what caused it," Clark said.

"Oh, no?" Dr. Carver noticed the shape on the floor covered with a white sheet. "What's that?"

"That would be Ray."

"And who is Ray?"

"My old boyfriend," Ellie said.

"I take it he's dead?"

"Yes." Ellie took a moment to explain how Ray died.

"I was afraid of this. Neither of you touched the body?"

"Only to throw a sheet over him," Clark said.

"Good. It's important you don't." Dr. Carver reached in his coat pocket. He took out a pair of blue elastic gloves and pulled them on with a snap. He lifted a corner of the sheet slowly and pulled it back, revealing Ray's smudged out face.

"How am I going to explain this to the police?" Ellie said.

"No one's contacting the police," Dr. Carver said.

"What are you saying?"

"That we're going to have to contain the body."

"What? We're just going to leave him here in my home?" Ellie said.

"No. We're going to have to move the body to the institute."

"But I thought you said we shouldn't touch it," Clark said.

"Would you rather we all end up in jail?"

"No."

"Then let's get cracking."

53

TRAFFIC STOP

The ice chest hadn't stopped shaking on the backseat of Dr. Miller's car ever since she left Don and Macy's apartment.

Glancing in the rear view mirror, Dr. Miller was relieved to see the lid was still sealed shut. So far the duct tape was holding, but it was only a matter of time before the adhesive stretched, creating even the thinnest of openings, big enough for the thing inside to squeeze its way out.

Dr. Miller looked at the dashboard digital clock and saw it was almost midnight. It was another five miles to the institute.

Once there she could easily smooth talk her way past the security guard.

But she wasn't sure if she would be able to get the emulator back into its tank all by herself.

She dialed Dr. Carver on her cell phone to ask for his help, and when it began to ring, she put her phone up to her ear.

A kaleidoscope of flashing red and blue lights shone in her rear window.

"Oh, no! Not now!" Ending the call, she tossed the cell phone on the passenger seat next to her purse.

The siren on the police car let out a curt whoop signaling for Dr. Miller to pull over.

Dr. Miller edged onto the shoulder of the road and turned off her engine. She glanced in the side mirror and saw the police cruiser pull up behind her car.

The officer left the headlights on and took a minute—probably to run Dr. Miller's license plate for any violations—before opening the driver's door.

The ice chest rattled in the back seat.

"Shut up!" Dr. Miller hissed, staring in the rear view mirror.

A tap on the window and a flashlight beam in her face startled her.

"Mind putting down your window?" the officer said, standing outside her door.

115

Dr. Miller nodded that she understood and smiled sheepishly. She pushed the power button on the armrest, lowering the window.

"Do you know why I pulled you over?" the officer asked, lowering the flashlight so it wasn't shining directly in Dr. Miller's face.

"Because I was on my phone?"

"No. You made an illegal turn. License and registration."

"Sure, Officer." Dr. Miller went in her purse and took out her driver's license from her wallet. She popped opened the glove compartment and retrieved her car registration and proof of insurance. "Here you go."

"I'll be right back." The officer returned to his vehicle.

The ice chest rocked and toppled forward, resting on the back of the front passenger seat.

"Will you stop?" Dr. Miller snapped. She was pushing the cooler back onto the rear seat when she saw the officer returning. She spun around in her seat and tried to look as normal as possible.

"I am giving you a citation," the officer said, handing her a traffic ticket. He shined the flashlight through the side rear window. "What's that?"

"I'm sorry," Dr. Miller said.

"What's in the cooler?"

"I just got a new fridge. I'm restocking my freezer."

"So what's with the duct tape?"

Just as Dr. Miller was trying desperately to think of a convincing reply, a voice sounded from the small two-way radio on the officer's shoulder. He turned away and tilted his head so he could speak into the microphone.

Dr. Miller couldn't understand what he was saying. All she heard was a bantering of police jargon between the officer and the dispatcher.

The officer signed off and turned back to Dr. Miller. "Have a safe drive home," he said and walked back to his patrol car. He turned on the siren, sped past Dr. Miller's car and was gone before she knew what was going on.

"Must be my lucky day," Dr. Miller said, staring in the rearview mirror at the ice chest in the back seat. She turned on her car's engine and pulled out onto the road.

Ten minutes later, she was pulling into the institute's parking lot.

Dr. Miller drove around and parked on the side of the building, figuring she would bypass the security guard in the front lobby and enter through the other entrance.

She grabbed her cell phone off of the passenger seat and was about to dial Dr. Carver when the driver's side door was suddenly yanked open.

Dr. Miller gasped when she looked up and saw someone dressed in black, wearing a ski mask. "What do you think you're doing? Who are you?"

Another person in similar attire, opened the rear passenger door and grabbed the ice chest.

"Sorry, Dr. Miller," the one standing closest to her said and zapped her with a Taser gun.

54

MUGGED

Stan McMillan slouched in the front passenger seat, trying his best to ignore the bag rustling in the cargo bed. "Are you sure it can't get out?"

"I'm not sure of anything, which is why we need to get it to the lab," Dr. Swanson replied, keeping her eyes on the road.

"Thank you for getting me out of there," Stan said, knowing if Dr. Swanson hadn't shown up when she did, he would have been arrested for sure by the cops at the market. "I swear, I didn't intentionally crush my boss' hand. It was that thing back there in the bag."

"I'm truly sorry, Stan. I had no idea it would react like that."

"What if you explain to the police it wasn't my fault?"

"I'm afraid I can't do that."

"Why not?"

"Because if I do, all my work will be for nothing and the institute will be shut down."

"But what about me? What am I supposed to do?"

"Try not to worry, Stan. I'll think of something. I just need time. Good, we're here," Dr. Swanson said, driving up to the front entrance of the institute.

Stan saw a security guard sitting at his post inside the brightly lit lobby, staring at the small screen on his cell phone. "Do you think it's a good idea going in this way? What if they have my picture plastered on the Internet?"

"You're right," Dr. Swanson said, and swung the car around. "We'll go in the side entrance."

When they turned to head down the side lot of the building, Stan saw a car parked just outside the lobby door. "Shit, someone else is here."

"That's Dr. Miller's car. What in the world is she doing here?" Dr. Swanson said, parking next to the other vehicle.

Stan got out while Dr. Swanson retrieved the emulator thrashing about inside the heavy-duty plastic bag. "You need a hand with that?" he asked. He looked at the stump on his right arm and almost laughed. "On second thought, never mind."

Dr. Swanson carried the bag over to the lobby door. The bag almost flew out of her hand when it slammed against the glass. "Will you stop!" she hissed.

Stan gazed through the passenger side of the other car. "Holy shit!"

Dr. Miller was sprawled across the console. She looked too uncomfortable to have fallen asleep.

Stan ran around to the driver's side and opened the door. "Dr. Miller, can you hear me?" He grabbed her shoulder with his left hand and gave her a shake.

"What's taking you?" Dr. Swanson asked, inserting her keycard into the reader.

"It's Dr. Miller. She's..."

Dr. Miller moaned and managed to sit up. She opened her eyes. "Stan? What are you doing here?"

"Are you all right?"

"My side hurts."

"Grab hold of my arm." Stan helped Dr. Miller out of her car.

"Wait, where's my purse? It should be on the passenger seat."

"No, it's gone. Looks like you were mugged," Stan said. "You're lucky they didn't carjack you as well."

"Oh my God! The ice chest! Don't tell me they took that too?"

"Where was it?"

"On the back seat."

"Not any more. Whoever assaulted you must have taken it." Stan walked Dr. Miller over to the side entrance.

"Doreen, what in God's name happened to you?" Dr. Swanson asked, as she stood waiting for them, propping the door open with her body.

"Never mind me. We have a serious problem."

55

THE THREE CONSPIRATORS

Libby opened the door and let Curtis and Sean into her studio apartment, the main living area aglow from the flickering dozen or more scented pillar candles positioned about the room.

Sean was carrying an ice chest, Curtis a woman's purse. They walked right by her, went into the small kitchen and put the cooler and purse on the table. Both men had their ski masks tucked in their back pockets.

"What's with all the candles?" Curtis asked. "It's like a mortuary in here."

"They're scented so you can't smell the litter boxes. What's in the cooler?" Libby said, joining them in the kitchen.

Four housecats paraded underfoot, some weaving in and out between the table legs or brushing against Libby's legs. A Siamese jumped up on the kitchen counter to get a ringside seat.

"Something Dr. Miller was transporting in her car," Curtis said.

"And she just gave it to you?"

"With a little persuasion," Sean swaggered, showing off the yellow Taser gun tucked in his waistband.

"My God, you actually shocked her?" Libby said.

"It's okay. He showed me how to use it."

"I thought we said no one was going to get hurt."

"Don't worry, she'll be *fine*," Curtis said.

"Should I go ahead and open it?" Sean asked, staring at the ice chest.

"Not yet," Curtis said. "Not until we're sure what's inside. For all we know, it could be dangerous. Might be why there's so much duct tape sealing the lid. What do you figure it weighs as you carried it?"

"I don't know, twenty pounds."

Curtis looked across the kitchen and saw a plump Persian sprawled on the floor and figured the fat cat was probably close to that weight. "Libby, what do you feed that thing?"

"Be nice. Trixie has a glandular condition."

"Yeah, I can see that."

"So what do we do now?" Sean asked.

"You're going back and getting that USB drive."

"You want me to go back to Ashley's house again? Why do we have to take all the risks?"

"Think it was easy sneaking into Dr. Swanson's office and copying her files; not to mention hiding that stupid memory stick in Ashley's purse?"

A yellow tabby jumped up into Libby's arms. "You seriously think someone is going to pay us a million dollars to get their hands on Dr. Swanson's research?"

"He said he had it all lined up," Curtis replied. "Hell, for all he knows we could get ten times that." He began rummaging through Dr. Miller's purse until he found some keys and a keycard. He glanced at his wristwatch. "It's almost two. While you're hitting Ashley's house, I'll see if I can get into those restricted rooms at the institute."

"And what am I supposed to do while you two are out gallivanting?" Libby asked.

"Stay here and guard that ice chest," Curtis said. "And whatever you do, *don't* break that seal."

"I won't," Libby replied, stroking her cat.

Curtis and Sean rushed across the room and went out the door.

Libby pulled up a chair, sat at the kitchen table and stared at the ice chest. "Hello, hello, anyone in there?" she said as though she were playing a childhood game.

As if in response, the cooler shook for a split second and went still.

56

MUCH NEEDED SLEEP

As soon as Stan and Dr. Miller stepped into the side lobby, Stan saw the three doors that led to the separate suites that Don, Ellie and he had occupied during their short stint at the institute. The thought of being able to lie down in one of those beds was tempting considering it had to be almost 3:00 in the morning.

"I don't know about you," he said to Dr. Miller, "but I could really use some sleep."

"Not until I get this into the lab," Dr. Swanson said, obviously having overheard him. She held the thrashing heavy-duty trash bag at her side as she swiped her keycard down a reader on the wall. The door lock disengaged with a loud click and she pushed her way through.

Stan and Dr. Miller followed her down a hallway. There were name plaques on the doors on either side of the corridor, signifying the doctors' offices. Dr. Swanson went to an unmarked door and opened it with her access card.

"Holy cow," Stan said the moment he stepped into the room with wall-to-wall aquariums. He looked inside one of the tanks and saw a shoal of jellyfish-looking creatures swimming in a circular pattern. "What are those things?"

"Those, Mr. McMillan, are what we used to replicate your hand," Dr. Swanson said. She lugged the heavy bag up to the top of a three-step stool, and dumped the salmon that had been on the chopping block at the market into the tank.

As soon as the fish plunged into the water, the emulators converged like a scourge of piranhas but instead of savagely devouring flesh, their tiny bodies assumed the shape, form, and characteristics of the salmon. There must have been a hundred miniature salmon the size of a man's thumb swimming determinedly in one direction like they were heading upstream to spawn.

"This is incredible," Stan said. He looked at Dr. Swanson. "You mean they can mimic anything they come in contact with?"

"Pretty much."

"So I have to ask: what went wrong with my hand?"

"To be honest," Dr. Swanson turned to Dr. Miller for her input but Dr. Miller only shrugged, "we're not really sure."

"That's it? You're not sure?"

"It's time we all got some rest," Dr. Swanson said. "If you'd like, you can use your old suite. Dr. Miller and I will take the other two. I think we'll all feel better after a few hours of sleep."

"I hope so," Stan said, still unsure if his life would be normal again.

57

PUNK IN A TRUNK

Ellie watched Dr. Carver and Clark wrap Ray's body up in the sheet and carry the dead man out to the yellow Mustang parked in the driveway and put him in the trunk of his own car.

"Okay, you two will have to follow me," Dr. Carver said, opening the driver's side door and climbing behind the steering wheel of the Mustang.

"Where are we going?" Clark asked.

"Downtown on the eastside."

"I thought we were going to the institute?"

"I changed my mind," Dr. Carver said.

"But isn't the eastside where all the gangs hang out?" Ellie said.

"That's what I'm counting on. Come on. We don't have much time."

Ellie and Clark ran out to the street and got into Clark's car. They followed Dr. Carver as soon as he drove by and headed toward the nearest freeway onramp. It wasn't long before they found themselves in a seedy area with overturned trashcans in front of rundown brownstones and abandoned vehicles with flat tires and smashed windows.

"I wish he hadn't dragged us down here," Ellie said, seeing a congregation of gang members up ahead, loitering outside a closed liquor store.

Dr. Carver laid on the horn and revved the engine as he passed by.

The hooligans whooped and yelled profanities.

A bottle was thrown, shattering on the street shy of the Mustang's rear bumper.

Dr. Carver lowered his window, stuck out his arm, and flipped the thugs off.

"Oh my God," Clark said. "Is he out of his mind?"

Dr. Carver gunned the Mustang and sped down to the corner and turned left.

"Cut through that alley so we can meet up," Ellie said, pointing to the dark thoroughfare between the buildings. She could hear the men shouting as they ran after the Mustang.

Clark accelerated down the alley to the next street.

Dr. Carver was already waiting for them on the sidewalk. He opened the rear passenger door, jumped in and hunkered down on the backseat. "Park across the street and switch off your lights."

Clark hung a tight U-turn and pulled up to the curb. He turned off the headlights but kept the engine running in case they had to make a quick getaway.

A few seconds later, Ellie saw the angry men storming down the sidewalk. They ran up to the Mustang, ready to beat the shit out of the driver, only to discover there was no one in the car.

A man with greasy long hair opened the driver's door and got in the car. He stuck his hand out the window and waved the car keys for his buddies to see.

The beefy engine fired up with a loud rumble.

Everyone piled into the car.

The driver stomped on the gas causing the rear tires of the Mustang to smoke as the high-performance car peeled rubber down the street.

"Think they'll bother to check the trunk?" Clark said, once the car was out of sight.

"Who cares," Dr. Carver said. "It's their problem now. Do me a favor and drop me off at the institute."

58

CURIOSITY CLONED THE CAT

Libby had been sitting for nearly fifteen minutes, staring at the ice chest, waiting for it to move again. Even her cats had picked up on her vibe and were curious of the mysterious container on the kitchen table.

Samba, her Siamese, had leaped onto the table to investigate while Goldie, her yellow tabby, remained in Libby's lap, gawking at the cooler.

Farina, the obese Persian, had managed to jump onto the chair next to Libby to get a closer look.

It was Misty, Libby's gray short hair, that proved to be the boldest of them all and was perched on the lid of the ice chest, clawing at the elbow of the duct tape securing the lid to the side of the container.

"Misty, you stop that!" Libby scolded the cat.

But Misty was determined and kept shredding away at the tape.

"I won't tell you—" but Libby never got to finish her sentence because the lid suddenly flew open and Misty was catapulted halfway across the kitchen.

The other three cats arched their backs and hissed.

Libby stared at the open ice chest. She could feel Goldie kneading her claws into her thighs. "Off," Libby said and upended Goldie onto the floor.

The cats began to yowl.

Libby wanted to flee the kitchen but she was too scared to move. It was as though she was glued to her chair. She craned her neck to peek inside the open ice chest but all she could see was about four inches or so of the white liner extending down from the rim.

Gathering her nerve, she inched up from the seat of the chair so she could see deeper inside the cooler. But when she stood all the way up— enough that she could see the bottom—she was shocked to see that the ice chest appeared to be empty.

"No, that can't be right." Libby reached over, grabbed a side handle, and pulled the ice chest towards her. There was definitely something in there; she could feel the added weight.

So why couldn't she see anything? Was it possible that whatever was inside the ice chest had camouflaged itself to blend in with the plastic lining?

Goldie jumped up on the opposite side of the table. The cat walked up, stood on its hind legs and leaned its head inside the cooler.

Suddenly a translucent tentacle reached up, looped around Goldie's neck and dragged the cat inside.

Libby heard a terrible screech as Goldie caterwauled and fought the invisible entity. She watched in horror as a geyser of blood-speckled fur spat out of the ice chest, followed by an ear-piercing howl.

The apartment suddenly became eerily quiet.

Libby watched a yellow head pop up. "Oh, thank God, Goldie. You poor thing."

Another head appeared.

Two identical yellow tabbies leaped from the cooler, upending the container and sending it crashing to the floor.

Libby cringed when she heard what sounded like a catfight erupting from under the table. She scooted her chair back to take a look and saw a yellow tabby splitting in half to create a newer version of Goldie.

Farina tried to run away but the fat Persian didn't get far when it was attacked and turned into a Farina replicate.

A vicious altercation broke out between Samba and a Misty look-alike.

Hair flew everywhere as the brawling cats attacked each other and multiplied.

Libby backed into the corner by the refrigerator and watched in horror, as her kitchen became a gladiator arena of savage cats, clawing and biting one another.

59

DROPPED CALL

This time when Sean climbed over the fence he made sure to stay close to the house so as not to trigger the motion detector spotlights in the backyard. He crept around to the patio, careful not to trip over anything that might cause a noise and wake up Ashley and her husband.

Sean inserted the thin end of the pry bar into the doorjamb of the sliding glass door, took a deep breath, and pulled back on the tool. This time the lock broke and the door popped open.

He stood for almost a minute and waited to see if he had awakened anyone, especially the dog. When he was satisfied everyone was still asleep, Sean slid open the door and stepped inside.

Holding the pry bar in one hand, he turned on his penlight and panned the room.

He was surprised to see two large fish tanks. Scanning the rest of the room, he went over to the desk, figuring the USB flash drive would most likely be in one of the drawers.

But after a thorough search, he came up empty.

He tried to think where else it could be. He knew he would be taking a chance searching the bedroom while Ashley and her husband were asleep. He noticed an empty dog pillow on the floor near the kitchen and knew their dog was probably in their room.

Sean knew Curtis would be pissed if after a second attempt, Sean missed yet another opportunity. There was too much money riding on Sean being successful.

Again, he scanned the room with his penlight. He stepped over to the fish tank across from the desk. He shined the beam into the water.

He saw something moving inside a hollowed out rock. An arm with an array of suction cups—*holy crap, Ashley has an octopus*—extended out and discarded a mussel shell onto the gravel bottom next to the USB flash drive sealed inside a clear waterproof bag.

Ecstatic, Sean took out his cell phone and called Curtis, who answered on the second ring.

"Yeah?"

"Curtis?"

"Yeah...what..." Curtis replied, his voice barely audible and breaking up.

"I know where the flash drive is. It's in the octopus tank. Curtis? Curtis, can you hear me? Damn," Sean said, realizing the call had dropped.

The hall light came on.

Ashley stood with her arms crossed. "Sean? What in God's name are you doing in my house?"

"You need to give me that flash drive."

"And I suppose you put it in my purse."

"No, that was Curtis," Sean said, realizing he had just exposed one of his co-conspirators.

"So, is Libby in on this too?" Ashley said.

Sean didn't comment.

"So what now?" Ashley said.

"I saw the flash drive inside the fish tank."

"And what if I say you can't have it?"

"Then I'll smash the tank," Sean said, raising the pry bar in his hand.

"No you won't." Ashley lunged at Sean, just as he pulled out a yellow Taser gun.

"Take another step and I'll—"

"The hell you will," Mitch said, suddenly appearing with his spear gun pointed at Sean.

Sean looked at the flash drive inside the tank and then turned his full attention at the trident tipped spearhead. "You won't shoot." He raised the pry bar, ready to strike the glass.

Mitch didn't hesitate and pulled the trigger.

The harpoon shot across the room, striking Sean in the shoulder, the bloody tip jutting out his back and pegging him to the wall.

60

CLOSE CALL

Curtis used Dr. Miller's keycard to gain entrance into the side lobby. It was the first time he had been in this particular section of the building. He saw a series of doors along one wall. He tiptoed to the first door and quietly opened it. There was enough subdued lighting from the lobby that he could see that it was a suite much like what he would expect to find in a reasonably priced hotel.

Dr. Swanson was wearing her street clothes and was fast asleep on the bed.

Curtis closed the door and went to the next room; a similar style suite. Dr. Miller was crashed out on the bed.

He checked the third suite and saw a man snoring, sprawled across the mattress.

He used the keycard to open a door leading into a hallway. Obviously, the card in his hand was a master and could unlock every door.

He searched the offices, starting with Dr. Swanson's, wondering if there was anything else he might find besides the files he had previously copied off of her computer. Once he was satisfied there was nothing else worth getting his hands on, he went to Dr. Miller's office and rifled through her desk drawers for anything of value he might be able to sell to anyone wanting to capitalize on Dr. Swanson's research.

Curtis had never been inside Dr. Carver's office before and was surprised to see a large fish tank inside the room.

When his cell phone suddenly chirped inside his pocket, he plucked it out and answered. "Yeah?"

"Curtis?"

"Yeah...what..." Curtis replied, recognizing Sean's voice.

"I know where the flash drive is. It's in the fish tank."

And then the call went dead.

What was Sean even talking about?

How in the world could the flash drive be inside Dr. Carver's aquarium when Curtis had personally put the memory stick in Ashley's purse?

Unless something had happened that Curtis was not aware of.

He figured it couldn't hurt to take a look.

There was a long stick lying on the stand, which he could use to probe inside the aquarium.

He slid the cover to the side so he could reach inside the tank. In order to touch the bottom with the stick, Curtis had to submerge his forearm partially into the water.

Curtis caught a glimpse of something jetting through the water.

It was an octopus, swimming straight for Curtis' hand.

The octopus extended its arms, wrapped them around the end of the stick, and gradually pulled itself up.

Curtis could see the beaked mouth opening as the octopus drew closer.

Suddenly, a hand grabbed Curtis by the shoulder.

"Curtis, what the hell are you doing in my office?" Dr. Carver yelled, thoroughly outraged. "Are you trying to steal Blueblood?"

61

BUSTED

Dr. Swanson awoke to the sound of shouting somewhere in the building. She rolled off the bed, slipped on her shoes and stepped out of the room just as the other doors were opening.

"What was that?" Dr. Miller asked, standing in the doorway, her hair mussed and her clothes all wrinkly from sleeping in them.

Stan stood outside his room. "Sounded like someone yelling."

"If I'm not mistaken, that was Dr. Carver," Dr. Swanson said.

"But what's he doing here?"

"I don't know. We better see what's going on." Dr. Swanson led the way to the door that connected to the offices.

Once they passed through and were halfway down the hall, Dr. Swanson could hear voices.

She stepped into Dr. Carver's office and saw her colleague confronting Curtis, one of her research assistants, standing in front of the fish tank. "Jason, what's this all about?"

"It appears Curtis has been ransacking our offices," Dr. Carver said.

"Is that true?" Dr. Swanson took a menacing step toward the young man.

"Hey, it's not what you think. I swear." Curtis was still holding the stick but had taken his hand out of the water.

"Don't lie to us," Dr. Carver snarled. "Who else is in on this?"

"Sean and Libby," Curtis volunteered.

"So who attacked me?" Dr. Miller said. "Was it you?"

"No, that was Sean."

"And where is Sean?"

"He's over at Ashley Sanders' house."

"At this time of the morning? What in God's name for?"

"To retrieve a USB drive with your research files."

"You hacked into my computer?" Dr. Swanson bellowed.

"Yeah, but then Sean called me and said the USB drive was in Dr. Carver's fish tank," Curtis said, shrugging his shoulders.

"Why in the hell would he tell you that?" Dr. Carver asked.

"Heck if I know."

"So where is the ice chest with the emulator you took out of my car?" Dr. Miller asked.

"We took it to Libby's apartment."

Dr. Swanson shook her head and yelled at Curtis. "Do you have any idea what you've done? How serious this is?" She looked at both Dr. Carver and Dr. Miller. "We have to get that ice chest back."

"Please, just let me go. I promise not to say anything."

"Not a chance," Dr. Swanson said.

"What do we do with him?" Dr. Carver asked.

"I'll watch him," Stan said. "Do what you have to do then you can decide later."

Curtis eyed Stan's stump.

"And don't get any wild ideas, jerk-off," Stan said. "I might have only one hand but I can still knock the snot out of you."

"We can lock him up in one of the suites," Dr. Swanson said.

"While you're dealing with him, Doreen and I will get the ice chest," Dr. Carver said.

"Come on," Stan said to Curtis. "Drop the stick and let's go."

Curtis was about to let go of the stick when Blueblood clambered up out of the water suddenly and latched onto the man's hand and bit him with its beak. Curtis screamed and shook off the blue-ring octopus.

"Ah, Jesus," Dr. Carver said.

Curtis grabbed his chest as thick saliva foamed from his mouth and he broke out in a sweat. Unable to breathe, he fell to his knees, threw up on the floor and collapsed onto his side. His body twitched like a fish out of water and then he was dead.

"I told you it wasn't a good idea to have that thing in your office," Dr. Swanson hissed.

62

NEWS FLASH

Clark sat at the kitchen nook, sipping his coffee while Ellie prepared two servings of eggs Benedict with rashers of bacon and generous helpings of golden hash browns.

"This looks great," Clark said as Ellie placed his plate in front of him on the table.

Ellie scooted into the booth beside Clark. She grabbed the remote control and turned on the portable TV on the kitchen counter so they could watch the morning news report as they ate their breakfast.

"Love this sauce," Clark said after forking a morsel of egg into his mouth.

"Some people like to use hollandaise sauce but I prefer Béarnaise."

"I can see why." He was about to delve back into his meal when he saw a badly mangled automobile wrapped around a telephone pole on the television screen. "Oh my God, Ellie, isn't that Ray's car?"

Ellie turned up the volume on the remote so they could hear the reporter, standing on the street, holding a microphone in his hand. Police cars and fire trucks were in the background, all lit up by the swirling red and blue revolving emergency lights.

"Last night ended in tragedy after a high speed pursuit of the suspects of a convenience store robbery," the reporter said. "Sadly, everyone in the car was killed on impact."

Ellie muted the TV and looked at Clark. "Does this mean we're in the clear?"

"Looks that way," Clark grinned. "When they find Ray in the trunk, the cops will think he was the victim of a carjacking." He turned sideways on the bench seat and stared at Ellie's face.

"What?"

"Those patches of scars you had around your eyes, nose and mouth. They've completely healed."

"They have? That's strange, I never felt anything," Ellie said.

Clark leaned in and kissed her. "I guess Dr. Carver was wrong. Looks like your immune system is working just fine."

Ellie smiled now that everything seemed to be resolving itself. "I know I should be feeling guilty, I mean I am the real reason Ray is dead, but to be honest, I'm not the least bit sad. Does that make me a bad person?"

"No, not at all," Clark said, wolfing down a mouthful of hash browns and washing it down with a gulp of coffee.

63

DO YOU SMELL SOMETHING?

"This should be Libby Brown's building," Dr. Carver said, parking on the street in front of the apartment complex. "What's her number?"

Dr. Miller looked at the slip of paper in her hand. "She's in apartment 33A."

They got out of the car and walked up to the main entrance. The front door was locked for the residents' protection. A panel of call buttons with the tenants' names was mounted on the wall next to the glass door.

Dr. Carver pushed the button for Libby's apartment. "Hello, Libby. It's Dr. Carver and Dr. Miller. Can you please buzz us up? We need to talk with you."

Thirty seconds passed and no reply.

"Maybe she left," Dr. Miller said.

"I'll try again." Dr. Carver pressed the button again. "Libby, are you there?"

Again, there was no response.

"What now?"

"This always works in the movies." Dr. Carver went down each row and pressed every button on the panel.

"What are you trying to do, piss off the entire building?" Dr. Miller said.

"Just wait."

"Yeah, what do you want?" an irate voice said over the speaker.

"Stop buzzing me," a man grumbled.

"Jamie, is that you?" came a woman's voice.

Dr. Carver pushed the corresponding button. "Yep. Let me in."

The door buzzed and the automatic lock disengaged.

"Well, there's one gal that's going to be disappointed," Dr. Miller said.

They entered the foyer and rode the elevator up to the third floor.

"This is it," Dr. Carver said and knocked on the apartment door.

When no one came to the door, Dr. Miller said, "Doesn't look like she's home."

Dr. Carver put his ear to the door. "There's definitely someone inside. I can hear some noise." He grabbed the doorknob and was surprised to find the door unlocked. He edged the door open a couple of inches. "Jesus, what's that smell?" He clipped his nostrils shut with his thumb and forefinger and stepped inside.

"Oh my God!" Dr. Miller said.

There had to be over a hundred cats in the tiny studio apartment.

They were everywhere, their shadows cast against the walls by the illuminating glow of the pillar candles situated throughout the room.

Mewling and purring, some of them hissing, while others screeched and clawed at one another.

Many pacing the floor like a moving carpet of fur.

Lying on every piece of furniture.

Perched atop the bookcase and refrigerator, sprawled on every flat surface. Walking on the kitchen table, the countertops, traipsing over the gas stove.

"Notice anything strange?" Dr. Carver said, still plugging his nose.

"You mean that Libby's one strange cat lady?"

"Yeah, well that too. No, the cats."

"You're right. There're only four breeds."

"So why all the same looking cats?"

Dr. Miller waded through the felines brushing up against her shins. "There's your answer," she said, pointing to the open ice chest lying on the floor. "They're replicates."

A score of cats had grouped together under the kitchen table.

Dr. Miller scooted a chair across the floor and spooked a few of them to back away. "Oh my God!" she shrieked.

"What is it?" Dr. Carver came over and saw Libby lying on the floor, half of her face eaten away. "Good God!"

"Jason, look!" Dr. Miller was pointing to a Siamese cat that was going through a transition, halving itself to create another identical feline.

"That's insane," Dr. Carver said, witnessing the hydra and jellyfish DNA portions of the emulator giving it the ability to clone itself as its molecular cells divided into a new regenerative creature.

Now that he was in the kitchen, he could hear a constant clicking sound. "Do you hear that?"

"Yeah, what is it?"

Dr. Carver looked over at the gas range and saw one of the cats tripping over a dial as it scrambled over the gas burners.

Dr. Carver took his fingers away from his nose. He took a deep breath and coughed. "Do you smell something?"

"You mean besides cat crap?"

"No, gas!" He looked around the room full of burning candles. "We've got to get out of here! This place is about to blow!"

They bolted out of the apartment and dashed down the hallway.

Dr. Carver heard a loud whoosh followed by a huge explosion. He could feel the scorching heat on his back as a fireball blew out the walls. He held onto Dr. Miller's arm and they kept running, avoiding the elevator and scampering down the stairwell, reaching the ground floor and racing out of the building.

They ran out into the street amongst the smoldering rubble.

"Oh my God," Dr. Miller said when she saw all the burnt cat corpses lying everywhere.

Dr. Carver stared up at the billowing smoke and the flames licking out of the blown out windows of Libby's apartment. "I never really was much of a cat person. Now I know why."

64

POLICE REPORT

Ashley was sitting on the couch with Dougie fast asleep on her lap while Mitch stood a couple of feet away answering the policeman's questions. An ambulance had been dispatched and the EMTs were wheeling Sean out on a gurney.

"I'll have someone meet you at the hospital," the officer said. "Until then, I would suggest you keep him restrained."

"Sure thing," the female EMT replied.

The officer turned back to Mitch. "So you know this man?"

"Not me. He works with my wife," Mitch replied.

"Any idea why he would break into your house?"

Mitch glanced over at Ashley and saw her shake her head. "No, not really," Mitch replied.

"Is it possible he has a thing for your wife? It's not unusual for a coworker to be infatuated with another coworker. Believe me, I see it all the time."

"Ash? What do you think?"

"If he did, I wasn't aware," Ashley replied.

"You really think if he had the hots for my wife he would threaten her with a Taser?"

"Maybe he planned to abduct her," the officer said.

"My God."

"Lucky for you, you were able to defend yourself. I have to admit this is the first time I've seen a homeowner protect his family with a spear gun."

"Yeah, well, I hope he's all right."

"Well, he did break into your house. That's a felony," the officer said. "We'll need the both of you to come down to the station as soon as you can so we can fill out a report."

"And until then?" Ashley said.

"We'll keep him in custody when he's released from the hospital." The officer carried the yellow Taser gun in the clear plastic evidence bag with him as he showed himself out the door.

Once she was sure the coast was clear, Ashley motioned to Harry's fish tank.

Mitch slid the cover on the aquarium, reached in the water, and grabbed the waterproof bag with the USB drive sealed inside. He shook off the excess moisture and handed it to Ashley. "I can't believe this was so important he had to break into our house. Good luck explaining this to your boss."

"Yeah, thanks."

65

BACK TO WORK

When Ashley arrived at the institute she was surprised to see there were no other cars in the employee parking lot in front of the building except for a couple of police cruisers, a dark two-door sedan and a black van with COUNTY CORONER stenciled on the side panel.

She parked her car three spaces away from the van and glanced at her cell phone to check her messages to see if maybe she had missed a notification from Dr. Swanson not to report to work, but there were no alerts.

Ashley shut off her engine, grabbed her purse and got out of the car. She walked along the sidewalk up to the front entrance and stepped inside the lobby.

Ralph Kennedy was standing behind the front desk with his hands resting on his utility belt.

Ashley approached the counter. "Where is everyone? Something happen?"

"Curtis Zane is dead," Ralph replied.

"That's terrible," Ashley replied.

"He was found in Dr. Carver's office. Apparently, he had broken in."

"That's strange."

"What is?"

"Sean Tanner broke into our house last night."

"What?"

"My husband stopped him. He's under arrest."

"Jesus."

"Is Dr. Swanson here?"

"She's in the back with the detectives."

"Can I go in?" Ashley asked. "I have something I need to give her."

"I've got strict instructions not to allow anyone inside. Is there something I can help you with?"

Ashley reached inside her purse and took out the USB drive. "It's very important that I give her this."

Ralph put out his hand. "I'll make sure she gets it."

"No, I need to give it to her personally."

"That won't be necessary," Ralph persisted. "I've got strict orders. Now, if you'll just hand it over." He made a beckoning gesture with his fingers.

That's when Ashley noticed something was missing on Ralph's gun belt—the yellow Taser gun. "On second thought, I'll come back later." She backed away, stuffed the USB drive back into her purse and hurried out the door.

66

OVER DRINKS

TWO WEEKS EARLIER...

Ralph Kennedy knew Sean Tanner, Libby Brown and Curtis Zane regularly frequented Palmetto Beach Bar and Grill after work at least three nights a week where they would get together and get hammered on Long Island ice teas.

Sitting at the bar, Ralph watched the three getting pleasantly buzzed in a booth in the back of the restaurant. Not wanting to be too obvious, he'd look in their direction periodically, waiting for the perfect opportunity to make his move when one of them made eye contact.

When Sean happened to glance his way and gave him a friendly wave, Ralph took that as a personal invitation. He grabbed his bottle of beer, laid some cash on the bar and sauntered over to the booth.

"Hey guys, mind if I join you?" he asked.

"Sure, have a seat. The more the merrier," Sean said.

Ralph squeezed in next to Curtis.

Libby acknowledged Ralph with a nod, slurping her cocktail through a straw.

He tipped his beer bottle in a salutation. "I hear if you suck beer up through a straw, you get drunk twice as fast. Sure cheaper than those mix drinks of yours."

"So how long have you been a security guard?" Curtis asked.

"At the institute, almost a year."

"Where did you work before that?" Curtis asked.

"You know, here and there," Ralph replied vaguely. He noted Libby's near empty glass. "Let me flag down the waitress."

A young buxom woman wearing a tight-fitting T-shirt and jeans came over and took their drink orders. When she left to go fill them, Curtis thanked Ralph.

"I'm just glad I don't have to drink alone. How pathetic is that? I take it this is your favorite watering hole?"

"Yeah, considering it's the only bar in town," Sean said.

The waitress returned and placed their drinks on the table.

Ralph paid cash, gave her a big tip and was rewarded with a great smile.

"So do you all work in the lab?" Ralph said, nursing his beer.

"In the main lab, yes," Curtis said.

"Correct me if I'm wrong, but isn't there a second lab?" Ralph asked.

"There is," Libby said. "But it's off limits. It's a special project Dr. Swanson has been working on with Dr. Carver and Dr. Miller."

"And that doesn't upset you?" Ralph said. "Being excluded. Sounds like Dr. Swanson doesn't trust you."

"What are you saying, sure she does," Libby said.

"We're her star lab techs," Sean boasted.

"Not from what I've been hearing."

"What have you heard?" Curtis said.

"She's hiring."

"Who told you that?" Sean asked.

"You'd be surprised what I hear when people come through the lobby." Ralph glanced over his shoulder and leaned forward on the table. "I heard Dr. Carver and Dr. Miller talking. That special project is going to make them filthy rich."

"What?" Curtis said.

"It's a shame you guys aren't part of the team. You might be looking at some serious money."

"Maybe we should talk with Dr. Swanson," Libby said, looking at Sean and Curtis. "What do you think?"

"If Dr. Swanson wanted us to be part of it, don't you think she would have asked us?" Sean said.

"What makes you think we haven't been? Hell, we do all the grunt work running those mundane tests day after day," Curtis grumbled. "What if she's been using the data we've been compiling; work that we should be getting credit for?"

Ralph glanced at his wristwatch. "Hey, I hate to drink and run but I have to go. Got an early shift in the morning."

"We should do this again," Curtis said.

"Sure, I'd like that," Ralph said.

"How about tomorrow, after work?" Sean said.

"Sounds good."

"Next time the drinks are on us," Curtis volunteered.

"Even better. See you then," Ralph said, scooting out of the booth.

He made his way across the restaurant and went out the door.

This was going to be easier than he thought as he walked down the sidewalk in the direction of his car. They were already disgruntled and seemingly gullible. He figured it wouldn't take long to persuade them to do his bidding.

But Ralph had lied. He wasn't doing this for the money and had no intention of making those three bozos rich; far from it.

He was out for revenge, pure and simple.

67

TOXIC AVENGER

Dr. Carver stood by his desk and watched while the detective who had introduced himself as Roberts oversaw the two men from the coroner's office slip Curtis into a black body bag and take him away on a collapsible gurney.

A uniformed officer came to the door. "Will you be needing us any further?"

"No, I think my partner and I can take it from here." By his partner, Roberts was referring to the other detective named Lanesboro who was questioning Dr. Swanson and Dr. Miller in a separate room.

Detective Roberts took out a notepad. He motioned for Dr. Carver to take a seat while he sat in the chair in front of the desk. "So you say Curtis Tanner broke into your office."

"That's right."

"But didn't he work here?"

"He did. So do Libby Brown and Sean Tanner. Curtis told us they were all in on it together and were planning to steal our research."

Detective Roberts consulted his notes. "Well, I don't think you'll have to worry about Miss Brown and Mr. Tanner anymore. She died this morning. Apparently there was a gas leak and her apartment blew up."

Dr. Carver acted surprised but didn't let on that he already knew because he had been there with Dr. Miller when it happened. "You mentioned Sean."

"He was apprehended in a botched burglary a few hours ago. You should be more careful who you hire."

"I'll say."

Detective Roberts shifted his attention to the large aquarium. "I take it that's the Toxic Avenger," motioning to the blue-ring octopus languishing on the gravelly bottom.

"I warned Curtis not to put his hand in the tank but he wouldn't listen. I still don't know why he would want to steal Blueblood; it's not like the animal is that rare or valuable."

"I'm sure we'll learn more once we question Mr. Tanner." Detective Roberts closed his notepad.

"What about Blueblood?"

"I'll let you know. Make sure the octopus is confined to the tank and don't allow anyone in your office. That should do it for now," Detective Roberts said. "Looks like these three won't be bothering you again." He got up and was about to walk out when Detective Lanesboro appeared in the doorway with Stan McMillan.

"Hey, Dr. Carver," Stan said. "I'm tired of running and have decided to turn myself in."

"What happens to him now?" Dr. Carver asked the detective.

"Dr. Swanson explained she wasn't aware at the time the mechanical hand Mr. McMillan had been fitted with had been defective and that his actions weren't intentional."

"I know I shouldn't have run off like that but it really freaked me out when I crushed Leo's hand," Stan said.

"It's possible the charges against Mr. McMillan will be dropped," Detective Lanesboro said. "Leo Turner underwent reconstructive surgery and should regain full mobility of his hand."

"Thank God," Stan said.

"Well, I guess that wraps it up for the time being," Detective Roberts said.

Dr. Carver waited until the detectives and Stan were gone before he went down the hall. Dr. Miller was sitting with Dr. Swanson in her office.

"What do you think?" he asked. "Pretty crazy?"

Both women smiled.

"Pretty crazy is right," Dr. Swanson replied.

"Well, at least now we can breathe a little easier," Dr. Carver said.

68

DOUGIE TO THE RESCUE

Ashley tried calling Mitch repeatedly at the house but each time the answering machine picked up. Figuring he might have gone down to the beach, she tried him on his cell phone and got his voicemail. "Come on, Mitch, pick up."

She drove straight home only to find Mitch's truck gone which meant most likely that Tony Delano had some work lined up and needed Mitch's help with the job. She made a call to Tony.

"Delano Home Remodeling. Tony speaking."

"Tony, it's Ashley. Is Mitch with you? I really need to talk to him. I've been trying to reach him on his cell but he doesn't answer."

"I'll get him. Give me a second, he's on the roof."

Ashley held on.

"Hey Ash, what's up?"

"I really need for you to come home."

"Can it wait, we're in the middle of a job."

"No, it can't."

"Here's the deal. I had to take the truck back to the shop. I rode out here with Tony. You'll have to come and pick me up."

"Where are you?"

Mitch gave her the address.

"I know where that is."

"Take your time. I'd like to finish the job so Tony can pay me."

"I won't rush, just be ready to go when I get there," Ashley said.

* * *

"So you think this security guard at your work is mixed up with the guy that broke into our house?" Mitch said, sitting in the front passenger seat of Ashley's Honda as they drove back to the house.

"That yellow Taser gun Sean threatened me with," Ashley said, "I'm a hundred percent sure it belongs to Ralph Kennedy as he wasn't wearing his this morning when I saw him. I could tell he was pissed when I changed my mind and didn't give him the USB drive."

"This might be a good time to give your boss a heads up."

Ashley pulled into the driveway and shut off the engine. "I'll call her as soon as we get inside."

They got out of the car and walked up to the front door.

The doorknob had been punched out and the jamb was splintered.

"Jesus," Mitch growled. "Not again!" He pushed the door and let it swing open.

"Oh my God," Ashley said, almost in tears.

Their house looked like it had been hit by a hurricane. Every piece of furniture had been toppled over, pictures ripped from the walls, a bookcase facedown on the floor.

Mitch's desk had been ransacked, the drawers and their contents scattered everywhere on the sopping wet floor because the glass on both of the aquariums had been shattered.

Mitch rushed over and searched Harry's tank. "He's not here." He went over to Dorothy's. "They're both gone!"

"*Where's* Dougie?"

"Oh, don't tell me. Dougie, here boy!" Mitch yelled. "Where are you?"

Ashley ran to the back bedroom while Mitch scoured the rest of the house.

When they met back, Mitch was furious. "He better not have hurt our dog."

"I'm calling Dr. Swanson," Ashley said. She was about to make the call when a sound stopped her. "Did you hear something outside?"

They turned to the sliding glass door. The entire pane had been smashed out leaving shards of broken glass all over the floor and out on the patio.

"Dougie, are you out there?" Ashley shouted and was answered by a short bark.

Ashley and Mitch crunched over the broken glass, Mitch nearly tripping over the ship's bell that had originally been on the bookcase as they went out onto the patio.

Dougie was standing in the middle of the backyard by the pond.

"Oh thank God." Ashley ran over and picked up the terrier. "You had us so worried," she told him and smothered his head with kisses.

"Well, I'll be," Mitch said, staring down at the murky water.

Ashley looked down. "How in the world..."

"Dougie must have carried them out here." Mitch got down on one knee and put his hand in the water.

The two octopuses swam over.

Harry touched Mitch's palm with the tip of one of his suction-covered arms.

"Will you look at that," Ashley laughed. "He just gave you a high-five."

69

HOME WRECKER

Ralph knew he should have just grabbed the USB drive from her when he had the chance but then there would have been a scene and the detectives were still in the back questioning the doctors.

Instead, he waited until she got into her car and headed out of the parking lot before leaving his post and running out to his SUV to follow her.

But then he'd lost her when she went through an intersection and he had to stop when the light turned red. Once it turned green, he sped after her though he had no idea where she had gone.

He went up and down the streets, finally spotting her car in a driveway. Parking further down the street, he watched her in his rearview mirror as she left her house. He figured the time it took for him to find her was enough for her to duck into her house and hide the USB drive.

Ralph got out of his vehicle and walked across the yard. He looked around to make sure no one was watching and kicked in the front door.

A small dog came running into the room the second he entered and growled at Ralph. "Get the hell away from me!" he shouted and went to kick the mutt. The dog avoided his boot and ran into the kitchen.

Ralph started with the desk and rifled through the drawers, taking them out one by one and dumping them onto the floor.

He turned and began tossing books off the shelves. He got so mad he pulled down the entire bookcase. A ship's bell clanked as it hit the floor with an avalanche of books.

He flipped over cushions and knocked over furniture. He marched into the bedroom, ransacking the room and found nothing. He could feel his anger gradually raging and desperately needed to let off some steam.

Ralph looked at the two large aquariums.

He picked up the ship's bell. He smashed the glass on the first tank and was instantly drenched from the knees down as the water gushed out onto the floor.

He turned and shattered the other tank.

"The hell with this!" He threw the ship's bell through the sliding glass door and stormed out of the house.

70

ALL ABOUT CYNTHIA KENNEDY

"So what happens now?" Dr. Carver said, sitting in a chair across from Dr. Swanson and Dr. Miller.

"What do you mean?" Dr. Swanson asked.

"I think it's time we take a step back; reevaluate the project."

Dr. Swanson slammed her fist on the arm of her chair. "No, out of the question! I'll be damned if I'm going to stop now because of a couple of hiccups."

"I'd hardly call them hiccups," Dr. Miller said. "You weren't in Libby Brown's apartment. Her cats were actually splitting apart to clone themselves."

"It's lucky for us they were all killed in the blast," Dr. Carver said. "Imagine if they had managed to get loose? The city would have been overrun by house cats."

"Better than a city full of rats," Dr. Swanson said.

"What's to say they would have stopped with cats," Dr. Miller said, "when they can assume any life form they come in contact with."

Dr. Carver saw the disapproving look on Dr. Swanson's face. "Just for now. Until we can figure out how we can control them. What do you say, Faye?"

"Maybe you're right."

"Of course we are. My God, Faye, three people are dead because of us."

"Three? I only know of two, Curtis and Libby."

"Sorry, I forgot to mention Ellie Phelps' ex-boyfriend. But don't worry. There's nothing to link his death to us."

"Is that right?" a man's voice said from the hallway.

Ralph Kennedy stepped into the doorway. He had his gun out of the holster and was pointing it at the three of them.

"What do you think you're doing?" Dr. Swanson said, rising from her seat but then planting herself back down in the chair when she saw the barrel of the gun angle her way.

"What I wish I had done five years ago. After what you did."

"Five years ago?" Dr. Carver said. "Neither Dr. Miller or myself were even working here." He looked at Dr. Swanson. "What's he talking about?"

"I have no idea," Dr. Swanson replied.

"Sure you do. Certainly you haven't forgotten my sister? Dr. Cynthia Kennedy."

A stunned look came over Dr. Swanson's face.

"See, you do remember." He turned to Dr. Carver and then Dr. Miller. "So I guess she never told you."

"Told us what?" Dr. Carver asked.

"That Dr. Swanson stole my sister's research."

"What?" Dr. Carver said. "Is that true?"

"Of course not," Dr. Swanson replied, indignantly.

"Then maybe you would like to explain how she died?" Ralph said.

Dr. Miller turned and looked at Dr. Swanson. "Faye, what's he talking about?"

"It was an accident."

Ralph scowled. "That's what you wanted everyone to think, but I know you killed her."

"What kind of accident?" Dr. Miller asked.

"It was in the lab," Dr. Swanson said. "She was bitten by a flamboyant cuttlefish."

"As far as our studies show, we've never used flamboyant cuttlefish," Dr. Miller said.

"Of course you haven't. She brought one into the lab for the sole purpose of killing my sister," Ralph said. "I was hoping to prove it and had Curtis sneak into her office and copy her computer files but the moron ended up losing the USB drive."

Dr. Carver stared at Dr. Swanson. "Were you really responsible for her death?"

Dr. Swanson had nothing to say.

"My God, Faye," Dr. Miller gasped. "Why?"

"Why do you think?" Dr. Swanson snapped. "Cynthia was hesitant to pursue the project and threatened to pull the plug. She said developing the emulators would be too dangerous."

"So you killed her," Ralph said.

Dr. Swanson smirked at Ralph. "No, the cuttlefish killed your sister. I only put it in the tank."

"Get up!" Ralph yelled, waving his gun. "All of you."

"Why? Where are we going?" Dr. Swanson said.

"I want to see them," Ralph said.

"That's not a good idea," Dr. Carver said.

"Shut the hell up! Everybody out! March!"

Dr. Swanson went out first followed by Dr. Miller and Dr. Carver.

"Keep going," ordered Ralph, taking up the rear, nudging Dr. Carver in the back with the gun muzzle.

When Dr. Swanson reached the door to the lab, Ralph told her to open it.

"Please, don't do anything you'll regret," Dr. Swanson said.

"What the hell?" Ralph blurted when he saw the jellyfish-like creatures in the aquariums lined up along the walls. He went up and tapped on the glass of a fish tank with his gun.

"I wouldn't do that," Dr. Carver said.

"Don't tell me..." but then Ralph was startled when he saw his face staring back at him from inside the tank.

He jerked back and the gun went off.

The bullet punched a hole through the glass causing spider web cracks to spread in every direction until the aquarium gave way like a ruptured dam and the water gushed out, dumping emulators all over Ralph.

He fell back in a panic, firing his weapon, each shot taking out more aquariums.

A bullet struck Dr. Swanson in the chest and she crumbled to the floor.

"Get down," Dr. Carver said and pushed Dr. Miller out of the path of the bullets, but in doing so, he shoved her into a tank that had been damaged and her head slammed through the glass. Dozens of emulators latched onto her flesh and immediately started to mutate.

Dr. Carver watched in horror as the creatures attached and mimicked the features of Ralph and Dr. Miller who were screaming in agony, their bodies transitioning into malformed replicates.

The ones covering Dr. Swanson were trying to duplicate her face but in doing so, the emulators had ended up looking more like half a dozen masks that had melted together. Two misshapen heads sprouted out of her shoulders.

Ralph dropped the gun and screamed when he saw five more fingers form on his right hand and his left wrist snap as another hand branched out from his forearm.

Dr. Miller lay facedown in the pooling water, parts of her dislodging from her body like evolving newborn creations.

It took less than a minute for the three separate entities to merge and become one entanglement of morphing bone and tissue.

Dr. Carver skirted around the thing amassing in the middle of the room and backed out into the hall.

Another tank shattered, then another, each releasing even more emulators to rain down atop the monstrosity. The gargantuan thing swelled into a hideous accumulation of extending body parts and began to squeeze through the doorway.

A giant crack formed and ran the length of the wall like a fissure parting the ground during an earthquake.

Dr. Carver felt something jab him in the small of his back. He turned and saw it was a handle on the door marked *Supply Room*.

He opened the door to the janitor's closet and saw metal shelves with gallon jugs filled with various cleaning products, degreasers, hand sanitizer, chlorine and ammonia.

Dr. Carver began removing the caps from the plastic bottles that he thought may be flammable liquids and began dousing the hallway, holding his breath so as not to be overpowered by the fumes.

He grabbed a couple more jugs of combustible liquid, spilling some as he went, and splashed the contents onto the giant blob oozing out through the door.

Frantically, he searched the shelves until he found a carton of long stem lighters used to ignite Bunsen burners. He took out a lighter, pointed the tip an inch off the floor, and pulled the trigger, igniting the incendiary pool.

The stream of fire raced across the hall and set the abomination ablaze.

An ungodly scream—like a tortured animal in unthinkable pain—reverberated throughout the corridor as flailing limbs turned into burning torches and the undulating mass became a raging inferno.

Dr. Carver watched in terror as the fire licked across the floor onto his shoes and rushed up his pant legs; the flames consuming him head to toe.

By the time the volunteers of the Palmetto Beach Fire Department responded to the call and arrived on the scene, the Bioengineering Clinical Research Institute of Medicine building was fully engulfed, leaving the dumbfounded firefighters nothing left to do but stand powerless and watch the entire structure burn to the ground.

71

DISAPPEARING ACT

Ashley and Mitch walked along the trail, each on either side carrying the large cooler by a handle. They wore their blue neoprene wet suits and water socks, Mitch with a beach bag slung over his shoulder.

Dougie was somewhere up ahead.

"You know I've been dreading this day," Ashley said.

"I know, me too," Mitch replied.

"What if you called them again, told them it was an emergency."

"I tried, but everything is on backorder. Besides, it's almost been a year. It's time."

"You're right," Ashley said, knowing the end of their life cycle was drawing near. "I'm just not good with goodbyes."

"Who is?"

They made their way down the steep path to the rocky beach below and found Dougie standing on a ledge overlooking the surf washing onto the rocks. No sooner would the seawater flow in, the outgoing tide would suck it back out again.

Mitch and Ashley found a calm spot on the water's edge. They set the ice chest down so it would float. Mitch placed the beach bag on a dry rock. He delved inside the bag and took out two scuba diving masks and snorkels, which they both put on.

With his mouthpiece hanging out, Mitch said, "Are you ready?"

Ashley nodded that she was.

They carried the cooler into the incoming surf. They walked out until they were waist deep, opened the lid and tilted the ice chest.

Harry and Dorothy slipped out into the ocean.

Ashley and Mitch submerged their heads underwater to watch the two octopuses.

At first they seemed unsure of their new surroundings until a strand of kelp brushed up against Harry and he took notice by feeling the seaweed with one of his suction cup-covered arms.

Harry was already changing color and the texture of his body, executing his ritual courting ballet.

Like a shy bride to be, Dorothy headed for deeper water, Harry following her to a secluded den of their choosing to copulate.

And just like the illusionists Harry Houdini and Dorothy Dietrich, the two octopuses performed the perfect disappearing act.

TO THE READER

I hope you enjoyed *NOT OF THIS WORLD: EMULATORS.* If you are interested in reading more of my books and have a proclivity for mutant insects perhaps you might like the *DEATH CRAWLERS* series or if you fancy cryptozoology there is the *CRYPTID ZOO* series, and the megafauna series *DEEP IN THE WILD.* For those of you that like Bigfoot, there are the *MOUNTAIN* books. And let's not forget those monstrous catfish in *SILURID.* If you prefer a novel about detectives investigating the macabre, might I suggest *IN CASE OF CARNAGE*? And if your partiality is short stories, please check out my horror collection *CREATURES.* Just thought I would throw that out there. Happy reading!

ACKNOWLEDGEMENTS

I would like to thank Gary Lucas, Romana Baotic, Nichola Tennick and the wonderful people working with Severed Press that helped with this book. It's truly amazing how folks who live in the most incredible places in the world can truly enrich our lives. A special thanks to my wonderful daughter and faithful beta reader (and accomplished artist on Fine Art America) Genene Griffiths Ortiz for her enthusiasm and making this so much fun. And of course, I would like to thank you, the reader, for taking the time to share these bizarre and incredible journeys with me.

ABOUT THE AUTHOR

Gerry Griffiths lives in San Jose, California with his wife and their four rescue dogs. He is a Horror Writers Association member. Gerry has over 30 published short stories in various anthologies and magazines, along with his own collection of 22 short stories entitled *Creatures*. He is the author of *In Case of Carnage: A Paranormal Crime Novel* as well as 23 novels published by Severed Press.

CHECK OUT OTHER GREAT DEEP SEA THRILLERS

SEA RAPTOR
by John J. Rust

From terrorist hunter to monster hunter! Jack Rastun was a decorated U.S. Army Ranger, until an unfortunate incident forced him out of the service. He is soon hired by the Foundation for Undocumented Biological Investigation and given a new mission, to search for cryptids, creatures whose existence has not been proven by mainstream science. Teaming up with the daring and beautiful wildlife photographer Karen Thatcher, they must stop a sea monster's deadly rampage along the Jersey Shore. But that's not the only danger Rastun faces. A group of murderous animal smugglers also want the creature. Rastun must utilize every skill learned from years of fighting, otherwise, his first mission for the FUBI might very well be his last.

OCEAN'S HAMMER
by D.J. Goodman

Something strange is happening in the Sea of Cortez. Whales are beaching for no apparent reason and the local hammerhead shark population, previously believed to be fished to extinction, has suddenly reappeared. Marine biologists Maria Quintero and Kevin Hoyt have come to investigate with a television producer in tow, hoping to get footage that will land them a reality TV show. The plan is to have a stand-off against a notorious illegal shark-fishing captain and then go home.

Things are not going according to plan.

There is something new in the waters of the Sea of Cortez. Something smart. Something huge. Something that has its own plans for Quintero and Hoyt.

CHECK OUT OTHER GREAT
DEEP SEA THRILLERS

THE BREACH
by Edward J. McFadden III

A Category 4 hurricane punched a quarter mile hole in Fire Island, exposing the Great South Bay to the ferocity of the Atlantic Ocean, and the current pulled something terrible through the new breach. A monstrosity of the past mixed with the present has been disturbed and it's found its way into the sheltered waters of Long Island's southern sea.

Nate Tanner lives in Stones Throw, Long Island. A disgraced SCPD detective lieutenant put out to pasture in the marine division because of his Navy background and experience with aquatic crime scenes, Tanner is assigned to hunt the creeper in the bay. But he and his team soon discover they're the ones being hunted.

INFESTATION
by William Meikle

It was supposed to be a simple mission. A suspected Russian spy boat is in trouble in Canadian waters. Investigate and report are the orders.

But when Captain John Banks and his squad arrive, it is to find an empty vessel, and a scene of bloody mayhem.

Soon they are in a fight for their lives, for there are things in the icy seas off Baffin Island, scuttling, hungry things with a taste for human flesh.

They are swarming. And they are growing.

"Scotland's best Horror writer" - Ginger Nuts of Horror

"The premier storyteller of our time." - Famous Monsters of Filmland

Check out other great

Sea Monster Novels!

Rick Chesler

HOTEL MEGALODON

An underwater luxury hotel on a gorgeous tropical island is set for an extravagant opening weekend with the world watching. The only thing standing in the way of a first-rate experience for the jet-setting VIPs is an unscrupulous businessman and sixty feet of prehistoric shark. As the underwater complex is besieged by a marauding behemoth, newly minted marine biologist Coco Keahi must face off against the ancient predator as it rises from the deep with a vengeance. Meanwhile, a human monster has decided he would be better off if Coco were one of the creature's victims.

Michael Cole

SCAR

Scar is a killing machine. Born from DNA spliced between the extinct Megalodon and modern day Great White, he has a viciousness that transcends time. His evil is reflected in his eyes, his savagery in his two-inch serrated teeth, his ruthlessness in his trail of death. After escaping captivity, the killer shark travels to the island community Cross Point, where prey is in abundance. With an insatiable appetite, heightened senses, and skin impervious to bullets, Scar kills everything that crosses his path. His reign of terror puts him at war with the island sheriff, Nick Piatt. With the body count rising, Nick vows to protect his island community from the vicious threat. With the aid of a marine biologist, a rookie deputy, and a bad-tempered fisherman, Nick leads a crusade against Scar, as well as the ruthless scientist who created him.

CHECK OUT OTHER GREAT DEEP SEA THRILLERS

THRESHER
by Michael Cole

In the aftermath of a hurricane, a series of strange events plague the coastal waters off Florida. People go into the water and never return. Corpses of killer whales drift ashore, ravaged from enormous bite marks. A fishing trawler is found adrift, with a mysterious gash in its hull.

Transferred to the coastal town of Merit, police officer Leonard Riker uncovers the horrible reality of an enormous Thresher shark lurking off the coast. Forty feet in length, it has taken a territorial claim to the waters near the town harbor. Armed with three-inch teeth, a scythe-like caudal fin, and unmatched aggression, the beast seeks to kill anything sharing the waters.

THE GUILLOTINE
by Lucas Pederson

1,000 feet under the surface, Prehistoric Anthropologist, Ash Barrington, and his team are in the midst of a great archeological dig at the bottom of Lake Superior where they find a treasure trove of bones. Bones of dinosaurs that aren't supposed to be in this particular region. In their underwater facility, Infinity Moon, Ash and his team soon discover a series of underground tunnels. Upon exploring, they accidentally open an ice pocket, thawing the prehistoric creature trapped inside. Soon they are being attacked, the facility falling apart around them, by what Ash knows is a dunkleosteus and all those bones were from its prey. Now...Ash and his team are the prey and the creature will stop at nothing to get to them.

www.ingramcontent.com/pod-product-compliance
Lightning Source LLC
Chambersburg PA
CBHW061236170626
46809CB00007B/2706

* 9 7 8 1 9 2 3 1 6 5 0 3 8 *